home is a verb

Kes Otter Lieffe

home is a verb

Copyright © 2024 Kes Otter Lieffe
Second edition published 2024 Berlin, Germany
ISBN: 978-3-949349-09-6

Editor: Thalie Barnier

Proofreader: Natalie Kontoulis

Cover designer: Eno Liedtke (https://www.eno-lied.de)

www.otterlieffe.com

dedication

I dedicate this story to the bird-loving elders who took me outside and taught me to listen.

And to the birds themselves who accompanied this writing—to the Charnecos and their flashes of morning blue, to the Wind-hovers who cause me to point and squeal *every single time*, to the Eisvögel and the Heidelerchen whose calls remind me to breathe, to the Dipper diving into cold water who made my heart leap, to the Eichelhäher who watched me write this dedication and to the tiger-striped baby Greenfinches fresh from the nest. And all the others, without exception. I love you, thank you.

acknowledgements

Over the two years it has taken to bring this work together, I've moved between habitats and communities; inspiration and grief; city and marsh; land and coast. Activist burnout and pandemic exhaustion have been my companions, but so have oceans and frog-song.

A list of those I'm grateful to, and who have helped create this work, will always be incomplete. Those who have supported this story in a thousand ways, the shifting community of friends and chosen family, humans and others, that I am so fortunate to be entangled with, landmates of all species, you are in my heart. We did this together.

Thank you to Clara, Freya, Nello, and Siân for your encouragement to keep writing. To Nicole, for everything. To Eno, for your creativity and vision in this beautiful front cover. To Thalie, for your clarity and gentle guidance in editing this story: I'm so grateful that this project brought us together. To dear Natalie, for once again bringing my wayward semicolons to order and reminding me how much joy can come from singing in water together. To Anja, my love, for your care and continued companionship. To S. Miller, you know why.

1. threat

prelude

An explosion in the sky above and I felt vibrations wash over me. Another drone crashed into the ground, launching blue sparks over dry grass.

I stood at the bunker entrance, trying to ignore the chaos and stay on task. My eyes blurred from the chemical smell as I squeezed thick industrial glue out of a dispenser and along the edges of the door. It was messy work. My gloves stuck together several times and the nozzle kept getting blocked. I wanted to do a good job, but these were all new skills, and my mind felt like it was on fire.

I finished and stepped away, not especially proud of my work. A friend moved in and continued sealing the bunker entrance with materials we had liberated from a DIY shop that week. I had never met this person before, but we were all friends that day. We were drawn by something more powerful than choice to do something unspeakable.

Another drone buzzed overhead. This one was armed, and someone shouted out a warning. My back was stiff and cold as I threw myself down into the dust of baked soil. We were exposed; surrounded for miles by open land with nothing except fences and bunker entrances. Someone appeared near me, lifted their gun, and took out the armed drone with the first shot.

I didn't carry a gun. Until a month before that day, I had never even seen one, except on TV. But we were here to kill and there was no point denying it. A drone is just a piece of electronics and engineering. The people down below the earth—as dangerous as they were—were human beings and we were sentencing them to a slow death.

The door was sealed, and a last layer of chains was secured around the entrance. It was the only part of the colossal bunker visible above ground, but I knew the grand tunnels and living spaces, swimming pool and storage chambers stretched out for hundreds of metres below us. I had seen the blueprints.

A friend I didn't know ran up to our little group. Her hair was damp with sweat and plastered over her forehead, and her pale, freckly skin was smudged with oil.

"Comms are down," she declared. "Antennas, dishes, we took out everything we could. There might still be some phone cables down there somewhere, but as far as we can tell, they were still setting up when they went down. They didn't plan this."

Unlike us, I thought. The people below us had retreated to their safe space in a state of utter panic. After unleashing terror on the world, after nature began to fight back, after the riots brought their reign to an end. Now they waited for their time to come again, in a billion-dollar bolthole surrounded by cans of foie gras.

And that's where they'd stay.

The friend with freckles led us out of the 'action zone' as we'd called it—as if we were trained soldiers and not cleaners, nurses and other regular, desperate, people. Kicking a smashed drone out of the way, I followed the others through the fence. When we had arrived just a few hours before, the barrier had looked so intimidating—five metres high and lined with barbed wire and security cameras. Now it hung at a strange angle full of holes chewed opened by bolt-cutters.

We set out into the yellow grassland as a group and I looked back, half-expecting dust clouds from security vehicles or the roar of a police helicopter descending, guns ablaze. But the landscape was still—the sky was white and empty, and the only dust was stirred up by our tired footsteps. No-one was coming to the rescue of the super-rich trapped in their hole. Their power had shifted. We continued walking for an hour and barely spoke a word.

At the edge of a forest, the group began to gather, and the atmosphere became suddenly electric. Some people shouted and cheered, others talked frantically, buzzing with adrenaline. One person started doing cartwheels on the grass. I sat down by myself and remained silent. I looked back at the land, heat shimmering over the horizon.

A tiny bird was calling and rising upwards in a perfectly straight line. *A skylark*, I noticed, one of my favourites. As I watched them disappear into the sky, I began to understand what that day meant—what protecting the earth truly looked like. We could no longer clear our conscience with organic parsnips and recycling, and we wouldn't want to.

Around me, people hugged each other in celebration. Someone was starting a fire to make dinner. Someone else spun around, their arms outstretched, face bright with elation.

I waited for the skylark to come back down. My head craned upwards, I felt dizzy. Breathing as slowly as I could, I tried not to throw up.

after

I don't enjoy revisiting the actions of that day, but sometimes it helps to channel the memories into stories. At least in the form of narrative, they have some meaning, otherwise they can too easily feel like intruders, hunting at the edge of my consciousness. I've learned that a story can be a container as well as a lesson.

The following memories are an offering, intended to help us all to understand the changes we went through during that time. The Shift, as we learned to call it, transformed us in ways that were both painfully dramatic and sometimes so subtle that I still struggle to understand what changed and what didn't. I have learned a lot since the days of the Bunker Blockades, and the years that followed, and yet, gaps remain. I've discovered that memory, for me at least, can be a deceitful companion.

In my recollection, life is a series of blurred out events with the occasional moment of shame remembered in perfect high definition. No matter how complete this version of reality might feel, I know it can't be the whole truth and I also know that my stories were never only about me. Perspective kills some of the pain.

But five years after the blockades, living alone on a beach, I had little of this insight. Without story to direct me, I was adrift in memories and only the daily tasks that defined my survival kept me tethered to the earth.

* * *

A familiar pain had returned to my shoulders. It had crept up unnoticed, brought by the sea wind and my hours sat in stillness. My neck was a series of cables, stretched so tight I could barely turn my head. A sharp stone dug into my ankles and my overgrown hair hung heavy and damp over my face.

I became aware of the pain in my left temple. It was a dull thud that came in waves, and it was always a bad sign, either that rough weather was coming, or that I hadn't eaten enough. Both were possible.

The land was overdue for a rainstorm. The wet season approached and each year it seemed to be heavier. More than the rain though, the weather that was sure to mess with my nervous system were the freak storms of dry lightning. They rolled in over the sea every few weeks, forcing me into my home for safety. The constant flashing was enough to bring migraines and I would throw up for days and nights without even the cooling relief of rain. Maybe it was that pain my body was anticipating.

I was also fairly certain I hadn't eaten since the day before. My last meal had been some left-over rice that was already turning. Living by myself, in the damp cave I had come to call my home, food was a constant struggle, and it was easier not to eat sometimes. Maybe that's what my teenage years had been preparing me for. Food had always been difficult.

I looked out over the expanse of blue-green water ahead of me. The waves were small and slow; only my mind was turbulent and unsettled. A bright white seabird—a gull or a tern, they were too far away to tell— dropped suddenly down into the water and re-emerged seconds later with a fish in their beak. My stomach rumbled.

I stood and headed back over the few metres of rock and sand that separated the sea, and all its unpredictability, from my tidy little cave in the cliff.

My home wasn't much, but I loved that place as if I'd built it myself.

Millennia of rainwater leaching through porous limestone had slowly carved out the perfect hollow; cool on warm days and sheltered from the rain with a stunning sea view. When I discovered my cave, I found the remnants of a bedframe and a shelf suspended from the wall—all set up ready for me to move in.

Who built my house and why will remain a mystery but months after the blockades and weeks after leaving the nearest town, walking with just my backpack, torn-up tent, and the most basic of supplies, I reached the end of the land and down below, nestled inside a calm cove, home was waiting for me to arrive. Several years had passed since then and when I had the choice, I never left.

At the entrance, I knelt down to the circle of pebbles on compacted sand where I laid my offerings to the land every day. The last crumbs of food had been taken away by the spirits—and crabs—and the small metal bowl I tried to keep topped up with fresh water had been half-emptied by thirsty sparrows and the warmth of the sun. I made a mental note to refill it when I could spare the water.

A line of large white stones demarcated the inside of my home from outside. I had brought the boulders there myself to create a symbolic sense of safety and they had served me well. I remembered the long afternoon it had taken to roll, drag and push the rocks into place, and the exhaustion and relief when I was done with my task. I remembered the storm who had rolled in that night and the difference I already felt, protected by my new guardians.

As I knelt there in the sand, I was drawn back into the land of memories: how smooth the transition from the moment. How tempting those familiar channels of regret.

My eyes stung from fire smoke. We sat in a circle, eating canned hotdogs and, following the elation of that afternoon, the conversation had become sparse and pensive. My legs and arms were tired—an emotional exhaustion I was powerless to prevent. I tried to smile and make small talk with the friends from the blockade, but my thoughts were of the people trapped below the ground. The wealthy and powerful locked up with their gyms and recycled water systems. I knew that they were people who had committed genocide and ecocide. That they had to be stopped by whatever means necessary. And I also knew, in the tightness of my chest, that they were people, as much human beings as those of us gathering to quietly celebrate their entombment. I remembered wondering how long their food supplies would last. How long until they began starving and turning on each other. How long until—

Food. That's why I had come to my cave. I needed to check if there was food left. I already knew the answer.

I stood and stepped through the guardian stones and walked the four metres to the back wall and the area I called my larder. It was a single rotting shelf of driftwood hanging from two knotted ropes that had welcomed me on my first day. The shelf was empty. The plastic supermarket bags that I had carefully suspended from it to keep food away from the ants, were empty too. Tied to juts of rock in the wall, the ropes were twisted blue plastic that still smelled like the ocean.

As a house made of literal trash, you might think my home was a mess. It certainly wasn't. My life was as tidy and hygienic as it had ever been. Every fourth day without fail, I brought new bracken leaves down from above the cliff to freshen up my mattress. Every morning I hung up my sleeping bag from another blue rope to air out: from the cave wall if it was raining, outside if it was sunny. Every sixth day I covered the latrine with sand and pebbles and dug a new one, two metres further along the beach.

A stolen water bottle—made for water coolers in some distant past of offices and jobs—would last two weeks if I was careful. I kept all the used bottles in a row in case I needed them one day for construction or storage. I wasted nothing.

Despite a lack of plumbing, my one pot, knife, fork and cup were always spotless. I had even managed to find an unopened pack of five brightly coloured kitchen sponges during a previous foraging mission and they had lasted me well. You see, home is very important to me. This is something I didn't realise until I lived for a while without one.

A shallow cave surrounded by screaming seabirds and itchy

sandfleas, occasionally flooded, and exposed to the caprices of the wind might not be everyone's idea of a perfect place to live, but I loved it the best I could. Also, it was easy to keep things tidy when there was only one shelf, and it was empty most of the time.

Standing in my larder slash bedroom, I began to process the lack of food, water—and pretty much everything else. Somewhere between that morning and the night before, I must have snacked on the last hunk of bread. The last apple had gone into the compost heap a few days ago. As far as I could remember, the bread and that almost-turning rice had been all I'd consumed for days.

I was usually meticulous at measuring out my rations—and making offerings when I could spare them—but my headache was getting worse. I wasn't thinking clearly.

I took my cup, filled it with some of the fresh water and poured it out into the metal bowl in the altar. I offered a silent prayer to the beings and the land I belonged to. I refilled the cup—the bottle was nearly empty now—and I took it with me to the edge of the sea. I looked out again to the horizon and between seabirds diving, thoughts of food, and the memories I had no control over, I made that precious drink last for an hour.

* * *

I am a bit ashamed to admit that I didn't eat again that day—or the next. It was only when my stomach really started cramping that I made the decision to go foraging. Sometimes I just don't like to leave home.

Maybe you've felt the same way. Home, wherever that might be, sometimes feels like the one place we can control when the world outside is chaos, danger, and unpredictability. I don't live like that now, but at that time, the gravity of safety, the inertia of staying still usually outweighed the desire, or necessity, of leaving.

And so I delayed as long as I could.

Although they came and went in waves, my headaches were getting worse. At one point I started retching but nothing came up except some yellowish water that spilled onto the beach. A curious young crab ran over immediately and began eating. I wasn't particularly disgusted, maybe a bit worried, and realised it was time to leave. Although I had barely anything to take with me and only one other set of clothes to change into, preparing to leave took a while.

I've always been good at preparing.

Years before this—when home had been a tiny flat in the city and not a sandy cave—stacks of canned food and ten-litre bottles of water lined up under my bed had literally kept me alive.

I remember a Tuesday night. My housemate, Adam, had had friends over for the evening. They were watching football on TV—which was still a thing in those days, for good or for bad.

Although Adam was sweet in a kind of innocent and simple way, his friends were a nightmare. I doubt a group of more clichéd, beer-loving jocks could exist in the world and I had been hiding in my bedroom the whole evening curled up with my microbiology books waiting for their little gathering to finish.

Finally, my bladder protesting, I put my ear against the door. As far as I could tell, they were all in the living room, the TV was blasting and I'm pretty sure one of Adam's friends was talking about dogs, or it might have been women. I decided to risk it and dashed out and across the kitchen towards our shared bathroom. Of course, they caught me.

"B!" one of them shouted in my direction. They all called me B back then. The jock stood in the middle of the kitchen, his clothes oversized and vaguely sports-themed. "Where've you been hiding?"

He was tall I noticed, and I would have found him hot if he wasn't disrupting my evening and my tidy house. For whatever reason he had opened almost every cupboard in the kitchen. I stood, frozen to the spot, looking, I'm sure, like a tiny, terrified mouse.

"You okay, B?"

I managed to nod and force a smile. "Just studying."

"Cool, mate, cool. Say, what is all this stuff?" he asked, indicating the open cupboard next to him. The cupboard was filled to the edge with bags of lentils and pasta. He pointed to another which held my secret stash of toothpaste, tubes neatly piled in stacks of ten, and several industrial-size bottles of hand gel. "Are you hoarding or something? I saw a documentary about that. This woman had like twenty cats—"

. I had no interest in the documentary or this person's perspectives on mental health.

"Were you looking for something in particular?" I asked as bluntly as I could although my voice still wavered. As stupid as I found him, this guy still had power over me.

"Corkscrew, mate."

I opened the drawer that was very clearly labelled for cutlery and kitchen implements—unlike all the cupboards he'd been poking around in—and handed him the corkscrew.

"Cheers. Join us for a beer? Half time's nearly over."

It was a demand pitched as a request and it all sounded awful. I mumbled an excuse, managed to escape, pee, and didn't emerge again until late in the evening to help Adam clean up the mess his friends had left behind. There was a chocolate stain on the sofa, a circle of wine on the carpet and a broken bottle on the balcony. I wasn't impressed.

Once order was restored, I retreated to my bed. It still felt odd in its new, higher position and there was less space between myself and the ceiling than I was used to. My room smelled of sawdust and plastic packaging.

The week before, Adam had helped me to elevate my bed by a metre to make space for the water bottles and giant bags of rice. He took my hoarding like most things in life: chilled and slightly detached. I had been prepping for years by that point, each week buying a few extra tins or a bag of coffee, spreading out the cost bit by bit so I wouldn't notice it in my budget.

Our walls were so thin, I could hear Adam making a phone call to his parents and later jerking off to some screechy porn. I knew he was even using headphones—as per our agreement—our building was just really badly built. There could be no secrets between us.

Apart from the occasional visits from his friends, living with Adam was easy and we were close. He was objectively cute and smelled good after a day at work, snuggled close to me on the sofa with a beer. But we never had anything sexual together. He was more like a little brother and after the first few times that he left the toilet seat up or put a stinking ashtray in the sink 'to soak', I knew it would never be more than that.

He teased me a lot, in a brotherly way. After a while of my obsessive stocking up, he started to call me 'Packrat', which I have to admit I didn't hate.

I was pretty sure I knew what was coming and that prepping was the best thing any of us could be doing. I was half-right. I was also half-wrong.

after

With preparation in mind, I got ready to leave my cave-home.

I cleaned the sand out of my rucksack and replaced it with the remaining drinking water, decanted into a plastic cola bottle. I sharpened my knife by scraping it at an angle, several times along the bottom of my saucepan. I have no idea when I learned to do that but thank God for survival skills. I retied my laces three times and then I went through what I had come to call my 'ritual'.

Three soft little touches on my bed, with my left hand, for comfort.

Three touches to my larder shelf to let my home know that I would soon bring new supplies.

Three touches to each of the five white rocks at the cave entrance. For protection and safety because that's exactly what I was leaving behind.

Some part of me was whispering that this wasn't healthy. Some part of me said it was fine and we do what we need to. Then without looking back—because I really can be disciplined when I want to be—I stepped onto the rocky beach I knew so well and headed east.

I had gone less than a hundred metres when the beach cliffs began echoing with my screams.

* * *

Pain shot out from my right ankle in every direction. In all fairness I probably screamed for less than half a minute before I caught myself, but it was a stupid risk, nonetheless. I gritted my teeth against the pain and tried to slow my ragged breathing. The agony receded enough that my brain could reengage.

My eyes focused and fell on the steep route I had started taking up the cliff. Barely discernible as a path, I had climbed and descended along the same line of rocks so many times that the grass between the stones had flattened over time. I knew every hand hold and convenient bush-branch to grab on to but that day a rock—who had looked perfectly steady—had rolled under my foot. My ankle had twisted. I had stumbled down to the beach. And screamed.

It hurt like all hell, and I felt a familiar sense of profound shame creeping up through my chest. I literally covered my eyes with my hands for no good reason but to hide from my own stupidity for a moment.

You're an idiot, I accused myself. You're better than this. I fucked up; I could die out here. Suck it up, keep moving.

The moment passed. Or shame pushed the feelings deeper inside. Either way, the pain became more manageable and I tried putting weight on my foot. It was slightly better than I expected. It still hurt, and I probably should have rested. Or elevated my leg or something. My stomach cramped; I pushed back my shoulders and took a step towards the cliff. Within a few minutes of careful clambering, I had reached the top. Without looking back, I headed north through a thicket of ferns, out towards the settlement. Although I had never seen a route of the area, my body—and instincts—knew the way.

before

I don't know if this is something special, but I'm really good at orientation. Adam, the sports-loving housemate with the terrible friends, was the exact opposite. He would use his phone just to get around our own neighbourhood and I never understood how or why.

For a while, Adam and I walked every day together along an industrial canal lined with bushes that were always busy with sparrows and blackbirds. I used to take the subway home from work until a particularly gnarly altercation with a couple of guys. Nothing too bad—and certainly not the first time—but enough that Adam had needed to hold me for half an hour on the sofa while I cried it out. Since that day, he came to my workplace every afternoon to take me home. He was sweet like that, and genuinely concerned. It also helped that his weed dealer was just around the corner from my lab.

This was a week before the first signs of collapse and a long while before the Shift—when life was still somewhat normal and included things like going to work and being groped on public transport.

"The sparrows are so fluffy now, they're getting ready for winter," I observed as we walked. The sky was overcast, and a cool wind was blowing.

Adam made a non-committal sound. How he managed to walk, play with his phone, and not fall into the canal, was amazing to me. It was also quite annoying.

"The swallows and swifts will be migrating soon," I offered. "We should take a trip out of the city some time to see the redwings when they arrive."

Another grunt.

"Unless the alligators arrive first obviously. Although I saw one in our shower the other day and it might already be too late."

Adam stopped abruptly and looked at me. "What?"

I smiled. "Doesn't matter. What are you doing on your phone anyway?"

"Getting us home."

I sighed quietly and we continued our walk. Adam liked the feeling that he was my protector, and I certainly didn't mind having a six-foot-four football player at my side, considering our neighbourhood. But I really didn't need him all that much—and certainly not to find our way home on a route I had taken maybe a hundred times. Also, it was literally a canal, where could we go?

Even if I've been to a place only once in my life, I know my way around, I know where everything stands in relation to everything else, and after the Shift that only became stronger.

I know that sounds like bragging, but it's not something I've worked for, it's just how I'm built. Knowing where I am on the land feels like an essential element of being part of it and when the land that I'm a part of is actual land—beaches and forest and marshes and mountains—not kilometres of concrete in every direction, that's easier to feel. But even in the city, it was a thing for me. I think I was always a bit more connected, but again, it's not something I chose, nothing to be proud of.

after

And so, without a phone—if they still existed in that time—and without particularly navigating by landmarks, I followed my instincts and made my way towards the settlement, to resupply my home. Concentrating on the journey helped me to ignore the throbbing in my ankle. I carefully followed a route that always stayed relatively dry although much of the land on either side was boggy marshland. I stepped into a patch of forest.

It was late morning, but under the canopy, shadows dominated. In another lifetime I would have been intimidated by the thick branches overhead, the shadows of curving roots and spikey bushes in every direction all around me. But I felt at peace making my way through the woods. Even if it wasn't as safe as my home, the forest felt like a place I wanted to be and where I could be myself. That wasn't the same before the Shift.

I moved out into an opening in the trees, a scruffy clearing left behind by industrial forestry. I was more exposed here and my gut and shoulders knew it. I moved slowly. The land was deep in regrowth and the ferns, bracken and brambles grew so high, I had to lift my arms above my head to avoid getting scratched. My shirt was already torn to pieces, there was no point trying to protect it, but a deep scratch on my body could take weeks to heal. And even if I had access, antibiotics were no longer a guarantee. I had to be careful.

Despite the danger, I browsed on blackberries as I walked. They weren't even nearly ripe but each one was an explosion on my tongue. Life reclaiming the land around me became as tangible as those acid berries. My skull hummed with cricketsong. The kisses of nettles burned my calves. There was a visceral power to the moment and my lungs ached to pull in every particle and second. A bird of prey circled above and for a moment I felt myself soar just as high.

My foot slipped on wet mud and sent a sharp pain through my knee. I was pulled back into distraction.

By taking this journey I knew I was making the injury worse. I also knew I had to keep going. With my headache deepening and the cramps in my belly, several forms of pain were vying for my attention. I vowed to rest when my task was complete. I promised to take care of myself so I wouldn't get sick. I pushed on.

$$* * *$$

My health has never been that good. Even back in my city days when I had much more control over my environment, I was sick a lot.

Part of me wants to reframe that, to tell the story of chronic illness as resilience, as adaptation and preparation for survival and isolation during hard times. It's not a bug, it's a feature; all along, pain was my superpower.

But honestly, it never felt like that. Sickness and pain weren't opportunities, and they weren't training me for anything. I would have done anything to avoid them.

Seemingly prone to infection by every virus, bacterium, fungus, and protist that found me, it felt inevitable that I would go into science, specifically microbiology. As my life, even in our sterile apartment, cycled through infection, inflammation, recovery, and exciting new infection, I grew ever more fascinated by the invisible beings that controlled my existence.

"Can I do anything?" Adam would ask, when I was laid up in bed for a week, burning through a fever, my muscles heavy and sharp and my mind a timeless fog of not-quite-over.

I didn't know how to answer. There was nothing he could do. How could he ever understand?

No-one seemed to get it. In those days I surrounded myself with people who were comfortable, and always had been, and that included people who thought being ill meant having a blocked nose for a week during winter.

There seemed to be two possible reactions to my perpetual sickness. One, it wasn't real; I probably wasn't trying hard enough. I should stretch and eat more turmeric. The second was harder to understand. In certain circles, disability was romantic and—most importantly—abstract, nothing like the corporeal and mental devastation I experienced it to be. It made me an alluring specimen.

When I came back to work after a week off, my colleagues would gush. I looked *great*, they would tell me. I was so *strong*. I'm sure they were secretly just curious about the microbes that had infected me. I certainly was.

Later, surrounded by middle-class, able-bodied activist types, with their hoodies and scuffed boots, being sick and poor became even more romantic. My immune-compromised presence became something to brag about. If I managed to get through all their access barriers, if I survived their filthy squats, toxic dishcloths, and four-hour meetings, I was celebrated as proof of the righteousness of the movement.

To be clear, pain is never romantic. Just like poverty isn't sexy except to those who have never been forced to count change and leave half their shopping and dignity behind at the checkout.

I know that infection might lead to immunological preparedness. I recognise that poverty has taught me survival skills that those around me were desperately short of. Overcoming obstacles *can* make us stronger and more resilient, and even—for some—inspirational. But a lot of the time, pain is just pain. It's exhausting and I would never choose it.

* * *

I stood, catching my breath. My hips were aching, my stomach cramped. Ahead, my route curved up a steep hill that I knew was the last obstacle between me and people. Beyond, lay the closest of the autonomous communities and therein all the supplies I could ever need.

A last push of energy and a determined bracing against pain and I began the climb. The steep slope was less vegetated, which meant it was easier to navigate, but also left me feeling more endangered with every step. *Which makes sense*, I realised in that moment. The people in the community weren't exactly my friends.

My chest ached as I reached the stand of a few dozen old pine trees who stood protecting the top of the hill. I stepped through them and paused at the other edge while my heartbeat slowed. I leaned against a rough trunk and took in the scene below me.

I stood at the highest point for miles around. The air was brisk and vitalising, but the land below was quiet. The settlement lay about one kilometre ahead, at a point between two worlds.

Ahead and to the north, flat, dry ground, lightly forested, stretched to a line of mountains on the horizon.

And beginning at the edge of the village, the wetland was dotted with ponds I had just travelled through. Apart from my little route—which I had memorised the day I arrived and never forgotten—the whole area was flooded marshland all the way to the sea.

A sparkling river traversed these habitats, crashing down the mountain in a series of massive waterfalls, then running over the land, out into the marsh, and down to the beach near my home. The river ran along one side of the village, seeming to protect and frame it. The riverbank was lush green grass where villagers sometimes lounged in the sun or had picnics.

Incongruously, a water slide hung over the river, suspended from the side of a raised platform in the trees. I had seen children jumping feet first into the tube of bright green plastic, to reappear moments later, splashing down into the deep water with great squeals of excitement. The whole thing had annoyed me at first. Noise and plastic stood at odds with this beautiful habitat. And what a waste of time and energy! In that moment though, I harboured other feelings. Envy for one. And a wish that I too could experience such freedom again.

I could smell freshly baked bread. I watched for several minutes, but no-one seem to be about. It was the hottest part of the day, and I knew from observation that most people would be up in the trees taking a nap.

I wondered about the status of the villagers sometimes. I guessed, and hoped, that they were all shifted. But it's not as though the non-shifted—or the Fittest as they called themselves—have glowing eyes or something so we can tell each other apart. Life isn't science fiction, even if it feels that way sometimes. And given how few binaries really exist in nature, I'm not sure that's even the right way to frame the question.

Once I was sure the coast was clear I made my way down the slope, stopping every few metres to crouch behind a bush to check again. The village seemed completely empty, but I knew that people were there somewhere, and to my traumatised brain, people always meant danger. I was hungry enough to risk it. Food was close.

before

Supermarkets were once a large part of my life in the city.

That seems not quite real when I think about it. I remember how overwhelming I found the bright lights and the droves of stressed people bumping trolleys into each other. I often woke up early just to avoid the crowds. The day of the riot was no different.

I arrived so early that I was among the first customers waiting as the workers—who looked even more tired than I felt—unlocked the doors. For the first ten minutes, I was practically alone with the tidy shelves and my steadily filling trolley. I entered a familiar trance of grabbing all my regular items, plus the carefully planned out extras for my preps. I tried, and failed, to block out the constant upbeat commercials on the radio.

Then, as I entered the last aisle, I began to notice how much the store had filled up since I arrived. The swoosh of the automatic doors had become more frequent and long queues had formed at the checkouts. Security guards began to appear, one at the end of each aisle. Their uniforms were scruffy, shirts not completely tucked in, as if they hadn't expected to be working today and had just rolled straight out of bed. The atmosphere in the supermarket was thickening, my shoulders felt tense.

I joined a queue. The eight people ahead of me—each with their own private mountains of toilet roll and bottles of cooking oil—were fidgeting and looking at their phones. They seemed to be intentionally avoiding eye contact with each other. I felt as if they knew something that I didn't and for a moment I wished I'd watched the news that morning instead of running out of the house so early.

I had barely moved one place forward when the first fight broke out behind me in the canned goods aisle. The fire alarm went off and made my heart leap. Police lights started flashing outside and a front window imploded. I abandoned my shopping and ran for the door.

When I came back the next day with Adam in tow, the supermarket had been emptied completely. It was the last time we would go shopping that summer.

after

Raiding the village warehouse didn't take long.

For several minutes I listened outside the supply tent. Then, holding my breath, as if that would help, I unzipped the entrance and stepped inside. My entire nervous system felt primed to run, or hide, or fight, if it came to that, but so far, I hadn't seen a soul.

I had no idea what would happen if they caught me, but I'm pretty sure the community knew *someone* was raiding their warehouses and kitchens. And yet, although they were obviously committed to protecting themselves, and often patrolled the village area armed with guns or sticks, the supply tent always seemed to go unprotected. It was almost like they wanted me to steal from them.

It was a large tent with metal shelving units lined with tins, bags of grains and eggs from the community chickens. I filled my rucksack with as much as I could carry and hefted it onto my back. I carried a sixteen-litre water bottle by the neck and stepped back outside. Above and all around me were platforms and huts: the supply tent was one of the only parts of the village on ground level. I headed cautiously towards the village square.

What I called the village square was more of an open gap at the edge of the settlement, connecting at one end to the river. It was often a hub of activity, and the grass was kept short by the sheer number of people walking across it. It was the last place I should have been going if I wanted to avoid people, but the communal tap was right at the centre, and I didn't know of another place I could fill up with fresh water. I stopped next to another tent and checked for people. Another push and I reached the edge of the field. I crouched down beneath a twisted hawthorn, their bark encrusted mint green with lichen.

This probably wasn't the smartest move I've ever made. It was at least a fifty-metre dash to the tap, and I knew I would be totally exposed. But as the throbbing in my temple reminded me, food and water are non-negotiable, and I had learned from painful experience that the water running in the streams closer to home wasn't clean enough to drink. I have no idea how the village filtered its water, but if it was good enough for them, it was good enough for me.

I slipped out of the straps of my backpack and placed it gently down on the grass. I took one final look around, picked up the big empty bottle and went for it. I dashed across the open space in a single breath.

The tap was rusted and squeaked as I turned it. The running water hitting hard plastic was loud and my body tensed. As the bottle filled, I looked around me as furtive as a deer who had hopped a fence.

Still nobody.

Bees hummed over the grass and the open field was hot from the sun. When the bottle was filled, I was almost tempted to let the tap water keep flowing. Into my cupped hands to take a long, quenching drink. Running over my head and arms, cooling me down. As hard as I tried to keep myself and my clothes clean, I knew that a good wash would do a lot for my mental health. I used to be so clean.

I pushed these fantasies away as quickly as they came and turned off the tap. Moving awkwardly with the heavy bottle in both arms held to my chest, I staggered back across the field to the hawthorn and placed the bottle down. It was just as I was wiggling again into my pack that I heard the snap of a twig from the direction I had come from and knew I had pushed my luck.

A person who I read as a woman was crossing the field with a rifle hanging across her chest. Her clothes looked as torn up as mine, but weirdly, I noticed in that moment how beautiful her eyes were in the bright sun—dark chestnut, I would call the colour. It's strange the things we notice in situations when we could die at any moment. Sometimes those are the images that stay with us.

Although distracted, I was perfectly still, half bent over with one backpack strap hanging over my right arm. Even my breathing had become shallow, and my chest was probably barely moving. I watched Chestnut walk across to the tap.

She poked at the wet ground with her bare foot then stood to her full height and, touching the gun lightly, turned to look around the field.

As she circled, I saw I would be coming into her view soon and immediately looked down at the ground, immersing my gaze into a small stone there.

This might seem like a strange thing to do. Surely, I would want to keep watching her in case she spotted me and started shooting? But since the Shift, instinct would take the reins sometimes and this was one of those moments. I wasn't fully in control. Looking back now though, it made a lot of sense.

I've learned that humans have many of the same instincts as other animals, among them a knowledge of when we're being watched. Although Chestnut might not actually see me hidden behind the tree trunk, her body, like all our bodies, was highly attuned to important information. Maybe her peripheral vision would unconsciously take in the whites of my eyes, or maybe she would have a feeling in her gut that something wasn't quite right, but my body knew that her body would know. And so, I looked down at the grass in front of me and at one point even closed my eyes entirely.

By the time I got up the courage to look again, Chestnut was already making her way back to the nearest rope. She fastened her harness to it and started hauling herself up to the platform above. As she disappeared into the trees, I felt my body shudder and my breath came in heavy.

I finally finished the motion of getting my bag onto my back. It was even heavier now. I picked up the water bottle in both arms and bush by bush, metre by metre, I left the community. Back through an unfinished section of the fence. Back to freedom and safety.

I climbed the hill in a blur, and it was only at the peak, hidden again amongst the pines, that I let myself sit down with a loud sigh. My hands were shaking as I hugged the precious bottle of water in front of me.

After a moment in which my mind was filled with visions of what could have been, I got down low to the ground, and tilted the heavy bottle just enough to bring the opening to my mouth. I took a sip and then another. And then a long gulp until I got myself under control and sat back up.

Okay, I thought to myself. It's okay. You did what you needed to do. And it's done.

* * *

The rest of my journey back home was uncomplicated. The water bottle had no lid, otherwise I would have preferred to roll it down the steeper spots of the beach-cliff. Instead, I struggled awkwardly and managed to aggravate my twisted ankle again. But I made it back, mission accomplished. The waves and salt-spray were a relief to my system. The cool solidity of my home was ecstasy.

And there I stayed for a few uneventful and sunny weeks. Waking up, preparing food, catching the occasional fish, and sleeping well. It felt wonderful to be back in my rhythm and in a place I felt safe. But change is the only constant, and the sunny days couldn't last forever.

before

I stood, staring into the portal of the washing machine, feeling grateful—for the tenth time that day—that our flat still had running water and electricity.

After that first surreal morning at the supermarket, the city had soon ground to a halt. As the superbug plague spread, people became scared to leave their homes. No-one was especially surprised. Antibiotic resistant *Enterococci* in supermarket meat, even organic meat, had been in and out of news cycles for a long time. *Gonorrhoea, Staphylococcus, Klebsiella,* one by one the resistant strains spread and became immune to all of our last-resort medications.

There was nothing new about this. As the life-saving magic of antimicrobials had been taken for granted and overused, the microbes themselves had been teaching each other to fight back.

But an unknown threshold had been passed and suddenly every subway seat touched, every package delivered, felt like a risk. A sneeze could be life-threatening, a scratch might never heal. The magic had been exhausted and industrial medicine was thrown back into the dark ages. First the hospitals became danger zones and finally so did everywhere else.

People said the lockdowns were like early 2020 all over again, but I was only a kid then. I remember that there were dolphins in Venice and Trump was evil, patents and anti-vaxxers made everything worse and it never really ended, even though we did our best to forget it. My parents were both killed in the first wave, and I moved into a foster home. Poor people didn't have a lot of options and there's nothing like a pandemic to expose the worst inequalities in society. I never forgot and when we became confined to our homes again, it felt like a continuation of a life full of crises.

As the plagues spread over the globe, food chains began to collapse—even in Western Europe, despite all our privileges. Governments urged the population to go out to work and companies threatened to fire anyone who didn't turn up to their shifts. Yet the fear of disease became greater than the fear of poverty and things unravelled fast.

As the weeks went on, Adam became increasingly grateful for my hoarder tendencies and never complained about them again. Over the next months as the situation got increasingly dire, we stayed in pretty much all day, eventually finding creative ways to exercise at home so we didn't need to go out at all. Adam's favourite was weightlifting with big cans of tomatoes. I stretched a lot on a second-hand yoga mat that had seen better days. We both tried Pilates for a while, but life is too short.

The supermarkets became too dangerous to enter and all the hand sanitiser in the world wouldn't have helped us against the bacteria or the mobs. By the third month we'd eaten nearly everything and were ready to kill each other, cooped up in that tiny space for so long.

As Adam joined me in the bathroom, I leaned against the washing machine, one hand on my hip, trying to appear relaxed while inside I was both raging and fearful.

"Adam," I whined. "Could you *please* take your laundry out when it's done? I don't actually want to be your maid."

My heart was racing. I don't even know why I got so wound up about these things—Adam barely raised his voice with me, even when he was really angry. I just hate conflict, even if sometimes I was the cause.

"Just leave it in the basket," he suggested, turning to end the conversation.

I knew that if I did that, it would be stinking by the time he got round to hanging it out. And if his clothes didn't get dry in time, there would be nowhere to hang mine. We only had one line and three metres wasn't nearly enough for all of Adam's football shirts.

I took the basket of his clothes to the balcony to hang them out, but for that to happen, I also needed to clear the line of his last wash. With a dramatic sigh, heard by no-one, I began to fold his clothes into a tidy pile and ball up what felt like one million pairs of white socks.

Adam joined me on the balcony and lit up a cigarette. He had only really started smoking during lockdown after losing his day job, and I hated the way the smell followed him around the flat now.

"You don't need to do that," he told me, carefully blowing a cloud of toxic smoke in the other direction. Despite his best effort, the wind blew it back over me and I supressed a cough.

"It's fine," I mumbled in a tone that I hoped let him know that it wasn't.

"Okay, if you're happy." He looked out over the busy street below our flat. A line of army trucks was crawling along; a patrol of some kind. "Doesn't seem to be getting much better out there. Do you know how much food we have left?"

I put down the underwear I was folding and looked up.

"Thirteen more days of three meals a day. Plus snacks and treats."

Adam looked surprised, although I didn't know if it was because I was keeping such a close eye on the stocks or because they were so low.

"I hope it'll be enough," he said and lit another cigarette. *Well*, I noticed, *at least he had the forethought to stock up on something.*

In the end, it was just enough; we left the flat eight days later. It wasn't completely safe, but we knew it never would be again and at some point, we just needed to re-join society—as changed as it now was. A new outbreak of *Strep* followed soon after. The weather oscillated between floods and droughts. There were so many far away wars that I couldn't really keep track anymore. The media described the new normal as one rolling crisis, and for some of us that felt like a description of life as we had always known it.

I have no doubt that my preps got us through that time. The alternative, as we saw every night on TV, could have been so different.

after

I had eaten well. I was hydrated. I had even spent an hour on the beach stretching, which is something I rarely make time to do. And yet, all day a sense of unease had followed me. It wasn't helped by the familiar shooting pain in my left temple.

The sky was perfectly clear with just a couple of tiny, fluffy clouds near the horizon. The lightest of breezes was coming in over the sea and the water was so still I'd even been able to watch a pod of dolphins breaching and hunting for a good part of the morning. Even now that afternoon was drawing in, there were no visible signs that a storm was coming, but I had learned to trust my body—and my body was telling me to prepare.

Okay, I'll get ready, I thought to myself. But what else was there to do? I walked around my home making my little checks. Everything that could be, was lifted off the ground in case the tide brought water in again. It had only happened once, but I learned very quickly that sea water and food supplies don't mix. I had already collected up the ferns and my sleeping bag and stored them in a little nook in the stone wall a few metres above the ground.

As I stepped back outside, I saw the stubby rowan tree who leaned out over my cave from the soil above. They were charcoal black, and I felt a heaviness in my chest each time I looked at their burnt trunk and branches. Water entering my cave was annoying, but the lightning that terrorised our region now was another level. And there was nothing I could do to prepare for it.

It hadn't always been that way. The area had become prone to electric storms abruptly over the course of a single year. Something had changed but meteorologists never quite worked out what. It was called climate chaos for a reason.

Increasingly, lightning would come even without a storm, just flashes and jagged spears hitting the sea, the beach, the forest, for hours—a grave danger for anyone without a cave to hide in.

The electric storms were so unusual, they had become famous. I remembered one time, a few months before lockdown, Adam had had a posh friend over for dinner. The friend—who had travelled way more than I found necessary—told us that the only place with more lightning was Lake Maracaibo in Venezuela. He used the moment to brag about staying in a four-star hotel there and watching the flashing sky from a bath of hot springs. I wasn't especially interested.

I stepped over to a boulder where my other set of clothes was completely dry after only an hour in the sun. It was supposed to be autumn. I folded carefully and stored everything in yet another plastic bag hanging from the top shelf. I did another loop of my tiny home to confirm that I had taken care of everything.

Then I made one final round to recheck the shelf, each individual rope, every plastic bag full of supplies, all secure. Then there really was nothing else to do and I went back to the beach to wait. The dolphins were playing again.

before

When lockdown ended, the real instability between me and Adam began. A survival mechanism had kicked in while we were trapped together that meant we were willing to resolve any conflict as quickly as possible because there was no way to escape the fallout. Without that we were doomed and a hundred and twelve days together is too much for anyone.

Adam was supposed to pick me up from work as usual, and he was late. Or at least I assumed he was late because I had been waiting for twenty-eight minutes and there was no sign of him, not even a message. I scrolled my phone relentlessly waiting for a notification.

Of course, I could have just walked home. Or even taken the subway if I really wanted to. But what if he turned up and I wasn't there anymore? What if he was hurt somewhere? I could imagine a thousand bad things that could have happened to him and what we'd need to do and who I'd need to call and… well, let's say that the few months leading up to that moment hadn't been helpful for my anxiety levels.

And then he was there, standing next to me. Grinning his stupid grin, his hair floppy and untidy. He smelled like sweat and tobacco smoke.

"'ello matey!" he said, affecting an accent that I'm sure none of his firmly middle-class family had ever had.

I crossed my arms and began to berate him. How could he make me worry like that? Why was he so thoughtless? Didn't he remember what happened to me with the sleezy guys—and their snarling pitbulls—on the subway?

His phone had run out of credit. He'd got caught up helping a friend with some emergency in her kitchen. He'd figured that I'd just head home without him.

I stopped listening.

"Adam!" I barked. He stopped mid-sentence. "If you say you'll do something, you really just need to be here, I don't know how else to say it. How many times have I asked you if you have enough credit on your phone? How many times have I lent you money so you can buy some?"

Even though you have rich parents and spend all your money on cigarettes, I thought but didn't say.

"I need you to show up for me once in a while."

Adam was incredibly good at what I called his sad-puppy face. I tried to ignore it as we walked home in silence. The rain started before we were even halfway home.

There was a moment, turning the corner into our street, when he pointed at a little flock of sparrows sheltering from the rain under a shrub. He smiled at me, and I knew he was trying to make peace. I continued to ignore him.

When we arrived at the front door, I slammed the wrong key into the lock and twisted it so hard it broke off. We stood for four wet hours in the wind before a locksmith came to let us in and install a new lock. The entire building had to get new keys.

For me and Adam it was the beginning of the end.

after

The storm arrived with a whisper. At first it was just a few gusts, bringing an almost imperceptible increase in humidity. My skin was charged and waves of goosepimples ran over my arms. My head throbbed and I tried to focus on the sounds of the waves and then the rhythm of my own breath.

Breathing in. I breathed in. My chest filled with air.

Breathing out. I breathed out. My chest released.

In.

And out.

My body stopped bracing.

Gradually the horizon between the sea and the sky grew darker. It was probably early afternoon; sunset wouldn't come for another five hours. And yet, the darkness spread. The clouds merged into a thick line that approached the coast.

My scalp prickled all over a microsecond before the first rumble of thunder reached my ears. A thick gust of air brought the smell of ozone and the first drops of rain, and I knew it was time to seek shelter.

My body didn't feel ready to withdraw completely. I crouched on one of the guardian boulders looking out as the rain arrived. Feet planted in the sand, elbows on knees, my chin resting on my hands, fascination pulsed through me. It hadn't rained for weeks. Lightning flashed and flashed again; the rain was growing to a steady pour. I realised that my headache had vanished without a trace.

Although protected by the overhang of the cave, the noise was becoming overwhelming. Surf pounded against the beach. My home echoed. And I knew the storm was just getting started.

At some point I noticed an escalation in the sheer weight of rain. For a minute, maybe two, I closed my eyes and tried to breathe through my own panic. My eyes and ears were buzzing, my chest was tight. I opened my eyes and looked back out over the dark beach.

A massive flash of lightning illuminated the sea for the briefest of moments and my heart leapt. I jumped to my feet and I gasped, maybe all at once. It must have been a trick of the light. Or fear was making me see things that weren't there. I could have sworn I saw someone outside walking along the waterline. *Towards my home. Towards me.*

I crossed my arms over my chest and strained my eyes to see through the curtain of rain and the premature night of dark clouds. Another shot of thunder crashed over me, and my hands went to my ears. Less than a second now separated light and sound. The storm was right overhead.

A spectacular flash and, this time, I was sure. A human-person was out there with something metallic across their chest that reflected the white light. And they were closer this time. One second later and soundwaves crashed down, almost knocking me backwards.

I had to get deeper into safety. I stood and turned and looked around my pitch-dark home, the after images of a human shadow against a white beach hanging in front of me.

My hands reaching out, I moved quickly across to the back wall. It was cool and damp; I put my back to it and crouched down to sit on my heels.

My mind was racing. I knew I should be safe in my home—and it would take a lot of determination for someone to come this far, especially in this weather. I had never, not once, seen another person nearby, not even on the beach. And yet they were here, and a cave would be a good place to sit out the storm.

My cave. Why were they here? Could it be someone from the village? Why would they come down to the sea today of all days? And what were they carrying? I didn't want to think that it was a gun, but I knew it could be.

My thoughts froze. There was a different sound. Almost impossible to pick out from the crashing and pounding of water but I knew my home. It was the sound of bare feet walking on wet sand. I searched around me in the darkness and my right hand touched something smooth. A rock.

I remembered exactly which one. I couldn't see at all now, but I knew the rock was grey and smooth with a vein of bright blue crystal running through. I had kept them there to brighten a dark corner.

I took my rock in my hand and unfolded my body until I was standing. My knees were slightly bent, my legs opened just enough to give me power and stability. My arm was braced, and my mind was quiet. I started running.

It happened so fast.

I have a recollection of another lightning strike. This one I actually saw hit the water. And I remember the smell of lavender—or rosemary—which seemed so incongruous I didn't know how to process it. The rest is a blur. My body was in control, there was only the moment: instinct and reflex, fight and defence. By the time I came back to myself, it was already over.

I was soaking wet, and a solid curtain of rain pounded down on my back. Beneath my knees, a person, face down in the sand. The sky lit up, less bright this time, and I saw my own right arm raised. The crystal vein caught the light, and it was red. Everything was red.

2. fight

after

I don't know how long I knelt there, on the beach in the rain, but time passed. I was rebooting: my thoughts were sluggish, my nervous system struggling to catch up.

I was aware that I was breathing. Which is a strange thing to notice, but it was the first sensation that made it through the fog. And I saw that everything was covered in blood—my hands, the beach.

I killed—.

No. The storm was passing. Okay, that was something I could actually process. I noticed that my beautiful stone lay in the sand and I was still kneeling on someone. A person lay face down beneath me. So much time without human contact and now, my knees were pressing into somebody's back.

I killed someone. The reality started to seep into my body. I could feel it moving through me as each organ and limb began to understand the truth.

I'm a good person. I had to defend myself.

I... killed someone. My stomach felt full of rocks.

As I rolled the body with slick fingers, I saw the beautiful features of Chestnut from the village. The cut across her forehead was deep and poured with blood. *I don't have that strength, this is impossible.*

The water from the cave overhang fell onto Chestnut's face in rivulets, washing the blood and sand away. The cut had stopped bleeding.

I now know the degree of shock I must have been in because it took me a good long minute to realise that Chestnut was breathing. Only when her eyes flashed open and she screamed intensely, pushing me away with powerful arms, did I realise that I hadn't killed anyone that day. But she might well want to kill me.

Chestnut stood up in front of me, then fell back down to her knees. Her hands went to her forehead and she looked at the blood she found there with disbelief.

"You...you...", I heard her say, but if she said anything else, I didn't catch it. I was already retreating into the deepest part of my cave, and my consciousness. I pulled my bed ferns down from their nook and tried to climb under or behind them, my back against the wall. It's ridiculous now I think about it, but I was *very* distressed and didn't know what else to do.

The sky outside was brightening. The rain had stopped and just the last drops of water were falling from the overhang. I saw Chestnut stand on wobbly legs. She rubbed her head again and then she stepped across the threshold towards me.

"You!" she shouted. I stayed silent. I'm ashamed to say I hid further under the ferns as if, somehow, if I just got deep enough between plants and stone, I could make this all go away. I willed myself to stop existing.

"I live in the village, and I came to help you," Chestnut said then. Her voice echoed slightly off the cave wall as she moved towards me. All I understood was "You attacked me... I'm... injured."

It had been a long time since anyone had spoken to me, and I stayed quiet. Peeking out between fern branches I saw that Chestnut was standing now, looking again at the blood on her hands. Only then did I notice that the metallic object across her chest was a pair of binoculars, now half-covered in sand.

She came to help me. I attacked her. She's injured.

Then Chestnut collapsed right in front of me on the sand floor of my tidy home.

* * *

After the storm passed, the next clear memory I have is of approaching the village, both of us sweating and stinking of panic. My right hand was somewhere above her right hip. Her left arm was draped over my shoulders. I took as much of her weight as I could as we stumbled forward through the brambles. Neither of us spoke and there was nothing to say.

We took the most direct route without going up my lookout hill. The worst had already happened, after all, and I needed to find other humans quickly. In so many ways my life was an independent one, but this was a situation I couldn't cope with alone. The sky was burning with the kind of sunset that can only follow the drama of big weather.

I heard calls from the village and a bell ringing out. We were soon surrounded by people who took Chestnut efficiently away from me and led her into a tent. I was left alone standing near the centre of the field. The communal tap was dripping and, numbly, I walked over to wash the stranger's blood off my hands.

∗ ∗ ∗

I woke up on an unfamiliar mattress, laying on my back. My blurred eyes took in dirty beige canvas a few metres above me. A single wren sang loudly, and the light through the tent walls was so bright that I closed my eyes again. I could smell something frying. It felt like morning. As my thoughts slowly coalesced, I noticed the pain radiating from my ankle.

I had twisted it again but no memory of that presented itself.

The crash of lightning. Iron-scented blood. Rosemary and pounding water.

The sensory images came rushing back. Laying alone, I refused to cry. Being stoic was a part of my survival strategy—crying wasn't helpful and if I started, I might never stop. But the sobs pushed up through my chest just the same. I may even have thrown up a little. It's still a bit foggy.

A while later, I heard a loud, upward, zipping sound as someone opened the door of the tent and stepped inside. I looked over in panic, my heart pounding. Chestnut's eyes were as beautiful as I remembered—even in that moment when they were filled with rage, and apprehension.

She stood at the entrance and the tent was large enough that she was still three or four metres away from me. I sat up in the bed. She unconsciously stepped back.

I'm dangerous, I remember thinking. *I hurt her.*

I started crying again. A part of me couldn't resolve what I had done, the role that I now occupied. *I'm a good person*, my mind was telling me. *I don't hurt people.* And somehow crying and being vulnerable seemed like it might solve everything.

Chestnut turned and left.

* * *

She didn't visit again for what felt like a few days, although without my rhythms and tasks, time had begun to blur.

I managed to leave the bed to use the bedpan. It was only a few steps away but the effort left me exhausted and in pain. Once in a while, a stranger from the village would bring food and water or empty the pan. I had no choice but to accept their kindness.

I didn't learn anyone's name. I had the sense that they wanted to leave the tent and get away from me as quickly as possible. I wanted to escape from them as well, but I knew how badly my ankle was hurt. It was an adrenaline miracle that I'd made it all the way from the beach.

Staring at the ceiling trying to keep my ankle as still as possible, I was bathed in the sounds of the village. Snippets of conversation and people calling to each other or exchanging news. The smells of a wood fire and children playing. Familiar gusts of wind arriving from the sea. And a painful absence of wave-speak over coarse sand.

I didn't want to think about home, the safety of my stone walls, the comfort of my quiet routine. The longing was so intense, I felt nauseated, even dizzy. I was on a cliff edge with no way to get back.

And I was lonely, I realised, although I was surrounded by more people than at any time in half a decade. That sense of being lonely, despite—or because—we're surrounded by other human people is encapsulated by one of my favourite Sasu terms: party-sorrow. There are opportunities to connect but we can't or don't take them. We're so close to being part of the group, but we're out on the edge.

Party-sorrow was an unfamiliar sensation for me and an uncomfortable one. There was a frustration to it, a sense of missing out. A craving for more than I had. I tried my best to push the sensations away and lay motionless in the tent as my thoughts and feelings continued to wander.

I remembered learning my first words of Sasu around the time of the Shift. I recalled the experience of resisting the new, while curiosity and need made me ache for more. Thinking about it, Sasu actually had a lot of terms for loneliness and aloneness— observation-retreat, connection-hunger—which made a lot of sense to me, given its origins.

My linguistic musings were interrupted by footsteps approaching and the sound of someone unzipping the door. I stayed perfectly still and feigned sleep. I didn't want to talk to anybody. I was scared, and honestly, I knew that the human-people in the village had every right to fear me as well.

"Hi."

Without looking, I knew it was Chestnut. Her voice was soft. I didn't respond; I didn't know how. A minute passed.

"I said, 'hi'," she repeated, more forcefully.

I rolled on to my side and carefully propped myself up on one elbow. I tried to reply, but the words got stuck in my throat. It had been a long time after all. My mouth moved silently, and I saw confusion, or something else, move across Chestnut's features.

"Can you speak?" she asked, a little softer.

"I... can."

That was it. Not much for the first words out of my mouth in however many years.

There was a time when I used to talk to myself or to the world around me. I would ask fish for their forgiveness as I took their lives for dinner. I would talk to my home at great length or to the sea. It was just kind of rambling or processing. But slowly, without making the decision, I'd fallen silent. Or my mouth had at least, my mind remained as noisy as ever. The conversations had simply moved inside.

Chestnut stood waiting.

"I can speak," I said, my throat clogging up a little as I pushed the words out. "I haven't for a long time."

She moved her weight and looked uncertain. "How long?"

"Four winters," I replied. The words were coming smoother now. "I've been alone since the blockades."

Chestnut looked surprised. "The Bunker Blockades?"

I nodded.

"I wasn't part of it," she told me, as if it was a confession. "But I have friends who were involved."

"Yes," I replied. Which wasn't the right response, but I was so out of practice. "I mean, oh, I didn't know."

She smiled then. It was the first time I'd seen her smile and I'm not exaggerating that it changed my world. "You *have* been away for a while."

"I have." I looked down at the ground intently. I could see a line of ants making their way from the table to the gap under the tent wall. "I...I'm so sorry."

I looked up and saw Chestnut's smile had evaporated. Her left hand had gone unconsciously to the bandage around her forehead.

"Erm...not yet," she said, bringing her hand down and placing both hands firmly on her hips. That seemed to make her feel more assured. "My name's Laguna. And you?"

"Laguna," I said slowly, relishing the sound on my tongue.

"Your name is Laguna too?" She looked confused again. "Really?"

"No," I said. "No, sorry..."

"You don't want to tell me your name?"

It was a fair question. We held names sacred in those days and sharing them implied trust. But if she had shared her name after what I had done, I felt obliged to do the same.

"Brook," I said. The word sounding both alien and familiar as it reached my ears. "My name's Brook."

"With an e?" she asked lightly.

What does that matter? I asked myself. I hadn't written anything down for so long I doubted I even knew how to anymore. And written language had ebbed in use for everyone, not just hermits living in caves.

"No e. Just Brook."

"Beautiful," she said, and my heart jumped. "I'll be back in a bit, Brook. I'll bring some food."

"I can get it!" I said as I pulled the sheet away.

I tried to stand, and it was as if my ankle wasn't even there. I collapsed onto all fours, my hands scattered tidy lines of ants, killing dozens at least. To my shame, Laguna had to help me back into bed.

"Rest," she ordered. And my body recognised the power in her voice.

I rested.

* * *

Laguna didn't return until the next morning.

An older person who I read as a man—although of course we can't know these things—brought me some bread and jam just after sunrise. I tried to say hello, or thank you, or something, but within thirty seconds, the person had shuffled away, zipping the door closed with slightly more aggression than I felt was necessary.

I mean, they could all just kick me out if they hate me.

As I sat up to eat, the pain in my foot reminded me that I probably wouldn't get very far. The bread was sourdough—heavy, salty and strangely familiar.

Because I've stolen it before, I realised.

And now here I was, benefiting from the kindness of these same people who I had plundered…and attacked. There was so much to feel guilty for even if I was just trying to survive.

Someone came to the door, and I could already recognise Laguna's footfalls. She paused for a moment before opening and entering. She turned and zipped up the door behind her.

"To keep the mosquitoes out," she said as if she needed to explain herself. "But I guess you're used to them, right?"

I was surprised when she walked over and sat at the foot of the bed.

"Can I get some?" she asked indicating the bread with her chin. I passed her the plate, and she broke off a piece and handed the plate back. Her fingers brushed against mine.

"It's tasty," I mumbled as much to myself as to Laguna.

"Do you like it?" she asked.

I literally just said that I did. I felt confused by this whole interaction, but I wanted Laguna to like me—or at least not fear me—so I nodded and probably tried to smile.

"It's okay," she continued. "Honestly, I like the other baker's bread more—it's not as salty and has more seeds, but this baker is learning fast. That's who came in yesterday and brought it to you. She's only been working with the bread for a few months."

"The older person?" I asked lightly even as a twinge of guilt made itself known in my gut. Some habits are so hard to break, even some as basic as assuming people's gender.

"Yeah. She'll share her name with you when she's ready."

"Of course."

Laguna softly changed the subject. "Sorry I couldn't come back yesterday. The filter broke down, and I was busy all evening with it." She paused, then pressed on. "You'd think with the amount of responsibility I have, I wouldn't still be unblocking slimy water pipes, but here we are. It was pretty urgent but—"

She fell silent and looked at the wall. She seemed embarrassed, as if she hadn't meant to share her frustration with me. Or talk to me at all, most likely. She scratched absently at the bandage around her forehead.

I couldn't understand why she would even want to be in the same room. Like many people, I blamed the Imperative for a lot of things in those days. Maybe it was that, maybe it was something else.

"Are you the leader of this community?" I asked, too abruptly.

Laguna's eyes went wide. She laughed but it came out of her nose and made a snorting noise. "We don't have leaders. We're shifted."

It was my turn to fall silent. In that moment, I couldn't see the connection between the Shift and whether a community would have leaders or not. There were so many things I couldn't understand in those days.

After a while I said, "Okay, me too. I mean, I'm shifted too."

"We know, Brook."

"Really?"

"Of course. That's why we've been feeding you for all these years."

*　*　*

"Feeding me?" My voice went higher, a sure sign of feeling defensive. I'd forgotten it did that.

Laguna smiled that gravitous smile again. "Did you think we accidentally left the supply tent unattended every time you popped by? Or that we just happened to store food on the ground when we have a dozen treehouses to keep it in?"

"I..."

"I know you thought you were being very covert coming down from the hill every time and sneaking around." Laguna moved her hands when she talked. "But there was no way that we wouldn't notice."

I stared at her for a long moment. I felt both ashamed and relieved.

The community had known about me and had let me get what I needed. When I thought I was most alone, I was cared for. Then Laguna herself had come to help me in the storm and—

"Laguna," I said, my voice more controlled now, as if I was trying to convey more seriousness. "I'm so sorry about what happened."

"With the food?"

"On the beach."

Her posture froze up for just the smallest of seconds, but it was enough to tell me everything I needed to know. She caught herself and feigned a more relaxed position. Her shoulders dropped; her chest opened, but I noticed that her right hand always returned to her left forearm, creating an invisible barrier of safety around herself. I know because I do the exact same thing.

"It wasn't your fault," she said. An edge in her voice made me not believe her.

My heart was racing. There were so many reasons I had left human society, but the stress of maintaining conversation was one of the strongest. The sea never disagreed or judged me during our conversations. And if I argued with my own thoughts, the consequences were limited. Well, not always, but it was a world away from speaking to another human. It always felt like such uncertain ground. Like, where would this verbal path lead? What consequences would there be? It's so easy to say the wrong thing especially when your brain doesn't work in quite the way that other people's do.

"I mean it *was* my fault," I countered.

"It wasn't. Well, not entirely anyway. You're shifted, inspired by the Imperative. That makes us act in unpredictable ways. I guess you sensed a threat to your home, and you reacted in defence. You probably don't even remember doing it."

That was all true.

"Look." She sat up a bit straighter and made eye contact. "I won't say that it was nothing or that it won't take me some time to heal. It will, of course. But it also wasn't close to being the worst thing that's happened in my life. I'll get over it, it'll be fine."

I realised my face was probably showing all kinds of emotions. Hiding those was yet another skill I'd forgotten along the way.

"Honestly, you feeling guilty about it isn't going to help me heal," Laguna continued. "There are other ways to make up for it if you want to. If you want to make reparations, it's up to you."

I nodded vaguely.

"I don't know what's happened to you in the past but please know that you won't be punished by me, or this community, and you don't need to punish yourself—although I'm sure you will and it's hard not to. Trust me on that."

I remained quiet, slowly processing what Laguna had said. It was more words and emotions, all in quick succession, than I'd had to digest in a long time. I was quiet for too long because Laguna asked, "Do you understand what I'm saying?"

"Yes, sorry, yes I understand," I said so quickly that I slurred the words together.

Laguna stood and stretched.

"How's your ankle?"

I wiggled my foot slightly and pain radiated up to my knee. "Still painful."

"We both have some healing to do," Laguna said with a philosophical tone. "If you need anything, just call out." She indicated the walls of the tent with both arms. "Most of us are up high but there are tents on both sides and someone will hear you and bring whatever you need."

"Thank you," I mumbled. Knowing that I was thanking her for much more than just that. "As soon as I'm better, I'll leave.

With a cryptic smile she said, "Just when you're ready and just if you decide to."

She turned and left me with my spiralling thoughts. As they so often did, my memories took me back to Adam; the friendship that carried us through a hard time and the terrible way that I decided to end it.

before

I collapsed into the sofa after a frustrating day at work. The bar of chocolate I had eaten on the way up the stairs hadn't soothed my nerves in the slightest. I was tired and grumpy, and the apartment smelled of fried onions.

"Coffee?" Adam asked loudly in that abrupt out-of-nowhere way that he always did. He walked past me, wearing only his boxers and socks.

"Thanks, I'm okay," I replied.

"I had another job interview today," he shouted from inside the kitchen. I never understood why he would try to start a conversation from another room. I made a point of not responding until he arrived next to me with a beer and flopped down into his grubby beanbag. "It was at the bank. I didn't get it."

He didn't seem particularly sad, but I made a sympathetic sound anyway. It was his third interview that week and though I was proud of him for at least trying, the economy was on fire, and I doubted he'd be able to get anything soon. Honestly, I wasn't a hundred percent sure there would even *be* banks for much longer.

Adam's parents were paying his part of the rent, which was at least something, but the rest was on me. Bills, groceries, not to mention the months of stockpiled food we had both lived on. And most of his tobacco and weed. It was starting to annoy me, but I wasn't ready to talk about it yet. I would keep pushing him to his interviews. And at some point, things had to turn around.

"Can I smoke?" he asked, reaching for a packet of tobacco on the coffee table.

I shrugged.

"Or outside?" he asked, and I was surprised that he'd understood me.

"Thanks, that would be great."

"No worries." He pulled himself out of the beanbag and stepped out of the balcony doors. He looked back at me, his expression earnest. "Oh, and Brook?"

"Mm?"

"I really appreciate that you're paying for everything round here. The second I get a job I'll pay you back for all of it okay?"

He stepped out onto the balcony.

* * *

The weeks drew on and I had been working longer hours to keep us housed and fed. Adam went to interview after interview with no success and I suspected that he was at least partially stoned in most of them.

He knew I was getting frustrated and tried to appease me by having dinner ready each night when I arrived home. He cooked like a six-year-old—and I will be happy to never eat macaroni and tinned meatballs again in this lifetime—but at least he cooked. I would have gone to sleep hungry otherwise.

One evening, three or four failed interviews later, Adam was on the balcony smoking as usual. Tired and anxious from too many long days at work, I decided, heart pounding, to confront him.

I should have prepared better. I should have been more forgiving. In the end, that conversation destroyed us.

"Adam, I'm trying to be patient," I growled at him as I stepped out onto the balcony. "But it can't go on like this. I can't keep doing everything around here, I need you to grow up a bit."

I could have used softer words and empathic listening. I could have gently highlighted the tensions I was feeling. We could have shared a beer and found positive ways forward together.

But Adam had a way of aggravating me in these conversations, and the angrier I got, the calmer he became. I knew he'd smoked half a joint, which just wound me up even more.

I was keenly aware that the neighbours could hear me, but I didn't care. *Let them listen*, I decided. *Let everyone know what I have to put up with.*

"Are you even listening to me?" His gaze drifted from me out over the city.

"I am," he replied. "But you really don't need to shout."

"How else will I get you to listen? How many times do we need to talk about this? How long do I need to spend all my wages on your tobacco addiction and your fifteen-minute showers?" I sighed and collapsed my shoulders. I was gripping the balcony wall so tightly it was making my neck hurt. "Look, Adam. I don't want to control everything you do. I want us both to be free, right?"

"Okay."

"But I also can't keep taking care of you forever. I have enough on my plate."

He turned to look at me.

"Brook." He said it so softly that my heart dropped. "I've never asked you to look after me."

I don't know why that was the line that broke me. Maybe it was because the implicit ask seemed so obvious—as far as I was concerned, without me, Adam literally would not survive.

Or maybe it was because deep down I knew in that moment that he really had never asked. That if I stopped babying him, he would find solutions just fine. That he actually wasn't my responsibility and that many things weren't. That sometimes I imposed myself on other people to fix their problems and then got frustrated when they weren't grateful or didn't respond how I would have. Between me and other people was a line that I had blurred to the point that I couldn't see it anymore.

It would take me years to work that one out. And in that moment, all I felt was defensiveness. Adam's truth burned.

Without another word, I stormed inside, went to my room, and slammed the door.

I lay for an hour stewing. I knew I was behaving irrationally. I was hurting Adam and he didn't deserve any of it. But as I heard him go into his room and start playing video games at full volume, I also knew that enough was enough. I had to leave; our time was ending. And it was my fault.

after

To this day, analysing my mistakes is something of a compulsion for me. To an extent, it helps me learn and to avoid infinitely repeating my missteps, but it's also easy for me to take it too far. I'm tough on myself, but I feel like I should be. Let's say I have a complicated relationship with fucking up.

I don't know how long I lay there in the tent in the village, but by the time I managed to emerge from all the repetitive thoughts and self-hate, the walls were turning orange. I had almost lost another day and it was time for me to get moving.

I pulled off the blanket and sat up. I placed my right foot down on the ground, carefully avoiding the ants this time. It was still painful, but I knew I needed to start exercising it or it would get stiff and that wouldn't help the healing at all. I pushed myself up to standing on my left foot and hovered there for a moment getting up the courage to try walking. I gently placed the injured foot down and slowly shifted my weight onto it. Pain shot upwards and I stumbled forward and grabbed the side of the tent. But it wasn't as bad as I was expecting. I could do this.

Something had fallen when I touched the wall. I balanced on my good leg, bent down, and picked it up. It was a walking stick; smooth, polished, and just over a metre long. I took it in my right hand and tried again. Much better. I took a few steps and made it to the entrance this time. Unzipping the door with one hand while holding on to the stick took some balance but soon, I stepped out of the tent where I had festered for too long and staggered out into the evening air and the community.

Although the tent was just made of canvas, I guess it had been protecting me more than I realised. The noise of the village was

55

overwhelming.

People moved everywhere, back and forth, carrying various buckets and plates and building materials and piles of folded clothing. It reminded me of an insect nest. I recognised the baker from before, carrying a big loaf of her heavy, salty bread. She gave me a weak smile as she walked by. I heard children squealing and splashing in the river. A dog was barking at another dog. People made their way over rough paths and others descended from platforms so high I couldn't see the top of them.

It was too beautiful, and it was too much. From between the tents, I could see the stand of oaks at the top of my hill, and I knew that beyond lay home and security. I started to walk.

Even with the stick, my right ankle felt...crunchy...and tight. The pain wasn't as bad when I didn't have to put my full weight on it, but I was already imagining the challenge of getting through the ferns and bracken with a walking stick and sprained ankle. And the cliff face down to the beach. It was intimidating, but I knew I didn't want to stay in this busy metropolis of human insects. *You're not built for this*, I told myself. *You need to get home.*

"Leaving us?" a voice inquired from behind me. I startled and stumbled on a clump of grass. Using the stick to stabilise myself, I turned slowly. It was Laguna, of course. My body had already become attuned to the tone of her voice and its gently rolling accent, which, I guessed might be Italian. She was wearing a different dress and her hair was pulled up into a ponytail.

She was giving me a strange look, which I was beginning to recognise. I had taken too long to respond.

"No...I mean, yes?" I replied.

Laguna actually chuckled. "You're cute," she declared. I had no idea what to do with that, so I smiled, my face muscles finding the gesture awkward.

"Why don't you join us for dinner first?" she asked.

"Okay. But then I really need to get home before dark." I looked up;

the colour of the sky was deepening.

"Of course," she said with a tone that my gut responded to, but my brain couldn't yet.

Why are humans so complicated? I remember asking myself.

You're a human too, I replied. On some level you must understand all this complexity. And it's not like fish and storms aren't all kinds of complex too.

But I find them easier to engage with.

I know.

I noticed that Laguna was looking impatient, she had crossed her arms.

"Thank you," I said, a little too loudly. "I'd love to eat together."

Two nights after the argument with Adam, I sat alone under a blanket, slumped over a plate of cold spaghetti, and burned fishfingers. The flat was quiet.

Adam had disappeared after our fight, and I hadn't heard a word. My body exploding with stress and anxiety, I had called too many times until he finally responded with a text message saying simply, "I'm okay. Staying with my family. Please stop calling."

I knew I had broken us. I'd gone too far and lost control and the guilt was overwhelming.

I know now that I wasn't alone in making these mistakes. I was accompanied, always, by exhaustion and trauma. It wasn't just me slamming doors and burning bridges, it was capitalism and scarcity and beautiful survival skills turned on the wrong enemy.

And still, there were so many other options.

I finished my spaghetti, ashamed that I hadn't found the energy to cook something better for myself. Eating food that would hurt my stomach the next morning also felt right, and I wanted the punishment. I drank two of Adam's beers and fell asleep in a stupor.

after

The food in the village looked incredible. I literally found it hard to believe.

It's not that I'd been eating so badly in my cave, but food has always been a challenge. Even when I had all the time in the world, my kitchen was filled from a recent raid and the wood was dry enough to make a good fire, it was hard to find the enthusiasm to slice things, cook them and then clean everything again afterwards.

Somewhere along the line I had gotten very good at gutting fish and though it saddened me each time to kill them, I did everything with as much respect and gratitude as I could. Not because I'm a great person, and certainly not because I grew up with respect for life as a part of my culture, but because the Imperative was so strong inside me, and it felt natural, and necessary, if I wanted to continue existing on this earth, to give something back. It was still a lot of cleaning though.

I already knew that this meal in the village would be on another level than I was used to. I was reminded of the miracles that could happen if food was designed for sharing and celebrating. And if the chef didn't have a probable, though undiagnosed, eating disorder.

The smells alone were enough to make me light-headed.

I stayed as far from other people as I could get away with and sat down in a plastic garden chair that seemed to have been intentionally left vacant. Some of the villagers sat in chairs, some cross-legged on the grass, others perched on logs. We were all more or less in a circle.

Apart from a few smiles or nods in my direction, people seemed content to let me sit quietly without interacting, which was fine for me. Plates were passed along the line and mine soon arrived, piled high with food more colourful, fragrant, and varied than I had seen in years. I closed my eyes.

Thank you to the beings who lost their lives, or offered their fruits, for this meal.

To the land that gave it and the people who gathered it.

To this food that will become a part of me. Thank you.

I opened my eyes and looked around me. Slowly each person opened their eyes and began eating with gusto.

We're not so different, I realised in that moment although I hated to admit it. *But I can't stay here.*

In retrospect, I should have known I wasn't going home that night. By the time we finished eating, the sky was already lined with deep purple clouds, and I decided not to risk it. I wasn't afraid of the dark and my sense of orientation was reliable, but with my ankle still healing and the exhaustion of all that resting, I decided to stay. Or, truth be told, it just kind of happened.

* * *

After dinner, I noticed Laguna leaving the circle. I imagined that she had some important village business to attend to, a meeting to run, a conflict to resolve. *Or maybe she just goes to sleep early.*

I gave myself a small tour of the village on the way back to my tent.

Even from ground level in the thickening darkness, I took in the buildings suspended above me, the gentle swing of the rope bridges and the bizarre unnatural twists of the waterslide. *How did they build all this?* I asked myself. *And why?*

I stepped around a pile of leaves. Stacked two metres high and contained within a vertical tube of chicken wire, the rotting material writhed with insects and worms. I had seen these cylinders scattered all over the village and they confused me. The leaves weren't even close to turning yet, so this must all have been saved from the previous year.

Some kind of compost? I wondered. *What is it all for?* I added it to my internal list of mysteries about the village that I never expected to solve.

My ankle was beginning to hurt again, and I returned to bed.

The sense of party-sorrow still lingered with me as I listened to the village sounds quietening down for the night. I slept barely a few hours when the uproar of humans and dogs tore me from my dreams.

* * *

Wolves. That was the first thing I could make out from all the shouting and panicked noise. Only they didn't say wolves, they said night-dogs—yet another lexical remnant left by Sasu. My Sasu was never that great, but it was enough to understand that we were in danger.

I grabbed my walking stick and made my way to the door. Which is strange, now I come to think of it. Normally my reaction to danger was to hide or to flee (or 'make a rabbit' as we called it in those days)—or even to fight if I really needed to.

But this wasn't that. I wasn't trying to escape by leaving the tent. If there really were wolves outside, it was surely safer inside—especially considering my new mobility issue. But I was drawn to help the others in the community and that force was more powerful than fear. *Fucking Imperative*, I thought to myself even as I unzipped the door and moved quickly out. It was a new moon and cloudy, but I could see well enough.

"How can I help?" I asked the first person I met. Even that didn't feel much like me.

The person didn't hesitate. "Grab anything you can use as a weapon and follow me to the fence."

I figured my walking stick would work and surely we were just looking for a show of strength after all. I am in no way equipped for actual combat with wolves.

I followed the person as quickly as I could, which was already much faster than that afternoon, to the edge of the village. The fence was maybe four metres high and mostly lined with barbed wire. Good enough to stop some night-dogs certainly.

But the barrier ended abruptly to the east with a five hundred metre gap before it started again. It was the same gap I had used as an entrance and exit point to the village. But half a fence was the same as no fence. I had no idea why the villagers hadn't completed it.

Why stop here forcing us to fill the gap with a new boundary of screaming humans? Was the sense of safety in the settlement just an illusion, I wondered. And if that was true, what else here wasn't real?

Villagers were lined up along the unprotected area on both sides of the stream, brandishing weapons of every kind from rifles to a kitchen mop. People were still arriving, descending quickly from the platforms above on ropes and ladders.

And beyond our line, I saw shadows. The night-dogs. I could hear them snarling, which is an insufficient word for that terrifying sound. Occasionally, one or two would appear from the trees near the stream and make a dash for the village.

The villagers responded with an uproar of shouting and waving. I found myself joining them although I didn't consciously choose to. I balanced myself with one hand against the end of the fence and slammed my walking stick down against the fencepost again and again. It wasn't loud, but in the collective, it was a roar.

One night-dog came close enough that I could see their eyes. *Devastating and beautiful,* I noticed, and my body was drawn to that energy even as I yelled to keep the danger at bay.

There were raised voices behind me and as I turned, I saw that people were running from the villages towards the fence. Their body language was pure panic and distress. Then I saw it, a night-dog, with something in their teeth, running at full pelt towards us. Our line scattered.

I saw that Laguna was leading the group of humans chasing the wolf out of the village. I had seen her emotional, but nothing like this. She seemed twice her normal size. I could practically feel the sparks of energy emanating from her form as she ran. The night-dog re-joined their people and the line of villagers closed back up to seal in the village and keep out the night.

The predators gradually lost some of their confidence—or interest. They had gotten what they came for. The snarls faded out and after a few more minutes, the pack of shadows withdrew to their forest and the energy of the village ebbed.

Laguna approached me. Her eyes were bright, and her breath came in pants. "Are you okay?"

I nodded. My breath was also heavy. "Do they come often?" Speaking still felt forced but the adrenaline and cortisol and fear that coursed through my body made anything seem possible.

"Often enough. They come down from the mountains. We have chickens and there are barely any deer left." She paused and looked away for a moment. "Last time they took six of our hens before we even realised that they were in the village. They're just really hungry."

Her right hand had found her left wrist and her shoulders were lifted as though to protect herself. I should have responded better, but instead I asked,

"And the fence? Why does it stop here? Why not complete it? Or just move everything up into the trees instead of half of the village up and half down? I *don't* get it."

It was the wrong thing to say, and I don't know why I thought I should be offering solutions. Her eyes flashed and I felt like I was looking at the night-dog again, locked into eye contact I couldn't escape. It escalated so fast.

"If *you* want to finish the fence, please do!" Her voice was suddenly loud. She took a breath but only so she could continue. "Maybe you have some barbed wire sitting in that cave of yours? That would be *awesome*. Really great ideas, thank you so much!"

I half-stepped back and just swallowed.

"Also—where would *you* sleep? Do you think you're the only person here who can't get up a tree four times a day? We *have* to keep some things at ground level. It was certainly convenient enough for you when you were raiding our food stores every month."

Laguna stared at me. I tried to look away but couldn't. Apparently, the sparks weren't only for scaring off invading wolves.

She exhaled loudly then pointedly turned her back to me.

Other villagers were gathered around us, they looked tired and curious. "It's over," she announced, her voice still loud but slightly more controlled. "Get some rest. And thanks everyone, this could have been a lot worse."

The villagers began making their way back to their beds. I wasn't sure if I should leave too, but Laguna stayed and so did I. I'm not sure I could have left if I wanted to. I felt rooted to the ground and had a familiar desperation in my chest; a desire to make it all go away. To hide or flee.

I swallowed and asked, "Are *you* okay? I'm sorry."

She stared at me for a few seconds. Her expression seemed conflicted.

"Yes," she replied, but her voice was still hard.

Laguna closed her eyes then. She inhaled and sighed loudly. Her shoulders dropped, and she looked at me again. Her eyes were softer. "Yes. I'm alright. Sorry, that was all a lot."

I nodded.

"Do you want to have some tea before we sleep?" she asked me.

It was an olive branch, and I took it with a small, awkward smile. After one final check that the night-dogs really were gone, Laguna led me back to the fire circle. We sat down on logs, and she poked at the fire.

The embers were still warm.

before

In the end, Adam and I didn't fight again. He came back from his parents after a week—carrying enough luggage for a month—and we slipped into a strange numbness. We barely spoke, and we began to make a concerted effort to avoid each other in the flat.

As far as I know, he stopped going to job interviews, or at least he no longer gave me his little reports on how they went. Most surprising of all, he finally started hanging up his own laundry. Then I knew it was serious.

He was out of the house a lot. His friends no longer came to ours, which I was grateful for, but it meant that I almost never saw him. One time he told me in passing that one of his friends—the jock who loved digging around in other people's kitchens—was sick in hospital from a superbug infection. I wanted to ask how he was doing. Was Adam worried about his friend? Was he sleeping enough? I wanted to take care of him and to break the ice between us. I wanted to hug and comfort him. Instead, I made small talk, went to bed early and killed the pain with a reality show on my laptop.

The moments we interacted at all, usually on the way to the bathroom or just as one of us was leaving the house, were awkward and cold. For weeks we cohabited like two people in separate worlds, so it felt like nothing more than a continuation when I told him I was looking for another place to live. He took it like he took everything those days, with a joint between his fingers and a distant platitude. He understood. He hoped I'd find something nice. And of course, we'd still be friends.

I didn't doubt he meant it, but his passiveness just hurt me even more. I missed him—being together in front of the TV or sharing a pizza on the balcony as a treat. Even the intimacy of surviving the worst of times together with canned ravioli and bags of rice. I missed our friendship, and I had no-one to blame but myself.

I found a new place in a week and packed my bags in less than an hour. Adam was out again with his friends, and I decided to leave quietly without a word or a letter. I held onto the door handle for a good two minutes to give myself the chance to change my mind.

I closed the door softly behind me, too numb to even say goodbye—to Adam, or the life we had shared together.

after

Laguna and I spent several hours together drinking tea and talking next to the fire. Although I knew I had upset her, if anything our emotional moment seemed to have brought us closer. Feelings are feelings. I'm sure it was a lot of work on her part, considering how awkward I still felt in these interactions. But she had a way of comforting me, and I began to feel more relaxed in her presence.

Once I had relearned the art of speaking to an actual human being, I remembered that it can be more than just fear and risk. I remembered how connecting it can feel to speak to someone of the same species.

I know that sounds weird. It sounds strange to me too, but it was very real. I could never know the experience of a crab or a moss or a river—the other-people as we would call them in Sasu—although I love them all deeply.

I could never know Laguna's life either, but it was closer to mine, it kind of had to be. And we were both shifted and that makes a big difference. Once it smoothed out, our conversation became dense, even a bit hurried, as if time was running out for us and we had just this moment to share everything we needed to know. Maybe we both sensed that the future couldn't be trusted.

I want to say that I patiently let her stories flow how they needed to, but she held such power while telling them, I couldn't have interrupted if I wanted to.

I learned that Laguna was five years older than me and had grown up in the capital. She had a big family but had lost contact when she came out. She didn't share many details about her childhood, but as a rule, I don't ask trans people about their families.

She told me some of her memories of adulthood in the city and how she had lost her job after her medical transition. She was unemployed for a while and ended up doing a job with a title I didn't really understand. Something in finance, she explained, which didn't clarify much. Then one day, in the sudden way that changes take place sometimes, after a trans friend died by suicide, Laguna decided she had lost one too many of her people to violence and poverty and she became an activist. She changed careers, started making some very different decisions, and dedicated her life to justice and creating something better. As far as I could tell, the Shift had just made that drive stronger for her.

I absorbed every word and gesture and facial expression as if preparing for a test. Deep into the night, over a third cup of stewed lemon balm tea, she asked: "And you? What was your life like? Before the Shift, I mean."

"I was a scientist," I told her and she looked surprised.

"Really?"

"I started as an intern. Then just after the superbug plague began, they bumped me up to an assistant in a microbiology lab."

"How was that?" There was a tone to Laguna's voice that I couldn't interpret.

"Erm...weird? I wasn't really qualified, and they recruited me straight after the lockdowns. I had a year left of my degree, but I guess they would take anyone who could operate an electron microscope at that point."

"And when was this?"

"Maybe a year or so before the Shift—or at least my part of it. As much as we can really measure these things."

I almost wanted to tell her about my personal experience of the Shift. How I had realised what was happening to me and the changes that followed. But Laguna changed the subject and for whatever reason we talked about Italian food for a while: I was a big fan; she was indifferent.

The evening was growing cold, and I wanted to stir the fire to get more heat out of the last embers. Near Laguna's feet lay a long branch that would be perfect for the job. Quickly, without thinking, I leaned over to get it. She jumped up so abruptly, she knocked her cup over, spilling tea onto the grass. She yelled, I yelled. We both ended up standing next to our fallen chairs, staring at each other, wide-eyed.

We both apologised—for whatever reason—and after a few seconds, took our seats again.

"I didn't mean to—I'm sorry," I mumbled looking at my feet.

"No, you're okay," Laguna replied. "My body is still..."

"Scared of me?"

"Kind of. It will take a while, Brook. Don't feel bad."

I poked my finger into my leg for a while. I couldn't think of anything to say. To this day, I'm still not sure what to do with those feelings.

"But anyway..." Laguna broke the silence and smiled as I looked up at her. "How do you feel about cats?"

That night we shared so much, and the conversation enriched me. And yet I was still missing the parts of her story that connected to the present. How had she come to the village? Was it already there when she arrived, or did she help create the community? Where did all the people come from and who built the treehouses?

She in turn didn't ask how I had ended up living alone in a damp cave eating stolen bread.

How could we begin to process any of that? It would take us a while to address the untold stories lurking at the edge of our fire time.

After a while, the conversation ebbed. Wishing me a good night, Laguna stood up and headed towards her home in the trees. I made my way back to my tent feeling pleasantly tired and dissatisfied at the same time.

before

Once I moved out from the apartment I shared with Adam, my days were mostly spent alone. I went outside a lot more. My new flat was so tiny, damp and mould-infested that being out of it felt like a relief and at least outside I could be around other people. The loneliness at home was unbearable.

Every day after work I took a long walk. Sometimes even *before* work if I managed to wake up early enough. Even in the heaviest of rain, I would head out, spacing out for the twenty minutes it took to reach anything that wasn't concrete, until I could watch other people playing with their cute dogs in the park. I was particularly fond of the small, wiggly terriers, although I never got up the courage to pet them or speak to their humans.

I was working a lot but always found the energy for my walks. I'd like to think it was the beginning of the Shift and the Imperative—that I was being pulled to connect with the living world of squirrels, crows, and bees. But I suspect it was more that I couldn't bear to be inside with my thoughts for a minute more than I had to be. I was alone in the city, and I missed Adam more than I wanted to admit.

We met for coffee about a month after I left. It was awful and uncomfortable.

I asked how he was doing—although I'm not sure any answer would have satisfied me—he said he was fine and had found a job in the post office. I said that was good. I almost told him that I was proud of him but knew how patronising it would have sounded. I told him I was doing okay too. Working a lot. At least the second part was true.

We promised to meet up again more regularly but never did. He invited me out with his friends, I made excuses and knew how hollow they sounded. He even sent me supportive messages every now and then, which I took weeks to respond to or just ignored. I chose the easy way out of the relationship and eventually he gave up.

It was a hard time for me, and I was going through a lot, but this decision—and it *was* a decision—to just fade away, was fragility, pure and simple. Although Adam would have gladly picked up the phone and restored broken bridges at any point, I knew deep down that I didn't want to be forgiven. I slipped into a life alone with a sense of inevitability and my long walks became the only thing I had to look forward to. Strolling among the trees watching woodpigeons flitting between branches above, for the first time I began to wonder why I was living in the city at all.

I woke up in my tent surrounded by village sounds. I was immediately restless. Although my ankle was still throbbing, I decided I needed to do something with my day.

As I stepped out of the tent, the first thing that caught my attention was the screeching *pii-yowww* of a sky-circler, hundreds of metres above me. I looked up but could barely see the hunting bird against the bright sky. Since the devastating collapse of most wild bird populations, predatory birds like sky-circlers had become much rarer.

They came to my beach sometimes and I had watched them soaring on thermals from land heated during the day, spiralling upwards as they searched for prey or carrion or a mate. I loved them, in the way that shifted people tend to love all living beings, but I didn't know them well. I had found a few feathers on the beach once and kept them among my precious objects at home, but otherwise sky-circlers were always too far away, in a life that didn't much overlap with mine.

I watched them continue their journey upwards until disappearing into the clouds.

It was then, my head facing to the sky that I finally engaged my senses with the hanging gardens spread out in the trees above me.

They were carefully maintained, intensely beautiful, and dominated the village. Yet it was as though I was seeing them for the first time.

I find that strange. How can we walk past something again and again without really noticing it—until suddenly we do? How is it possible for our senses to be so distracted by our thoughts that we can ignore the beauty around us? Now that the sky-circler had drawn my attention upwards, I began to realise how much I had been missing.

Practically all the available space in the trees had been given over to growing herbs, vegetables, and colourful fruit. Along the sides of the platforms above me, cascades of flowers hummed with bees. Up the walls of the aerial huts where the villagers lived, vines and peas sprawled vertically upwards, heavy with fruit. One large wall on the back of a hut had been turned into a strawberry nursery—at least thirty plants were laid out in tidy rows, each one nestled in their own pot-hammock, sending out stems, flowers, and tiny red fruits into the air. Even from where I stood, the air smelt sweet.

There were gardens at ground level as well, although there were fewer of them. I could imagine why: the land was so flat here and the weather so unpredictable, one good flood could wipe out everything in an afternoon. And so the villagers gardened as they lived, high up in the trees—at least for the most part. There were a good number of people working on the gardens that morning and I decided to join them, if only to watch and learn.

I had never really gardened before. Growing up in the city, and living most of my life there, it just wasn't a part of my world. Later in my home on the beach, I had no need for a garden because everything I needed had come from the sea. It hadn't taken me long to learn to fish, to catch crabs, even the occasional octopus. And certain dried seaweeds made an amazing salad, pre-salted. I enjoyed learning to feed myself from the sea and was proud of being able to meet my own needs.

I stood for a moment, gardens all around and above. I watched people working hard in various states of undress, sweating in the sun. Even the kids were active in the gardens above, on their knees on the platforms digging roots out of boxes of soil or collecting tomatoes from plants trellised up living walls.

I realised then that this story I had been telling myself—that I had learned to be independent and survive by my own means—was incomplete. I had had no autonomy while I was stealing half my food from these people.

That thought motivated me. I wanted to help out and get my hands dirty.

I chose a bed on ground level. I stepped over and picked up a tool. I didn't know what it was called: a long stick with a metal bit on the end that points backwards. I watched a villager who was working with the same kind of tool on a different bed. They lifted it high, let it fall back down under its own weight into the soil and then dragged it over the surface towards their body, scooping up weeds along the way. Later they collected the pile of weeds and threw them in the path to dry out. It didn't seem so hard.

Copying the villager's wide-legged stance, I got to work and started digging up the tiny weeds in my bed. After maybe thirty minutes or so I was covered in sweat, my bare feet were muddy, and my arms were tired. I had piled up a good number of plants in the path and my heart pumped with satisfaction. I like tasks that feel like cleaning.

I looked up and saw Laguna moving towards me. Moving *quickly* towards me. Her face was flushed and as she got closer, I realised she was also shouting.

"What the *hell* are you doing?"

I stood perfectly still as if maybe she wouldn't notice me and would keep on walking. She stopped right in front of me.

"Well? What is this?" She put her hands on her hips. I already recognised the meaning of that gesture and took a half-step back.

"I'm...weeding?"

"This whole bed is spinach and beetroot." She waved a hand over the piece of earth that looked so clean and tidy now—to my eyes at least. "And even some radishes. You must have killed a hundred of them."

"I...I didn't know."

I saw her catch herself then. It's a strange phrase but there was an actual jerk in her body as her mind and her body caught up with each other. I watched her while she took a few deep breaths. She closed her eyes and I just waited.

"Brook..." she said as her eyes opened again. Her voice somewhat calmer but still with an edge. Frustration? Disappointment? It was like the night-dogs all over again. I hated making her angry.

"—I'm sorry." I just kind of mumbled it and wasn't sure she heard me.

She got on her knees and started collecting up the tiny seedlings I had so brutally attacked. She looked up and gave me just a hint of a smile. "Let's see what we can save."

I remember musing how someone could switch so quickly from rage to calm. Was she just really good at pushing down her feelings? For someone like me who has always wanted to have more control over myself, and ideally over some of the outside world too, Laguna's composure struck me as some kind of superpower. My gut ached with a pang of envy. It would take some time until I realised that indeed it came from her power but not in the way I expected.

I kneeled next to her. "Can you show me how?" I asked softly, still a bit in awe.

The smile grew.

* * *

That night, resting by the fire after a long afternoon of undoing my mess in the garden, Laguna and I finally talked about the Shift. The village was quiet and everyone else had gone to bed hours before. A lone nightingale was singing with all his power from a willow. Laguna was holding a cup of nettle tea in her right hand, which she waved around as she spoke.

"It's funny, you know?" she declared, or asked, her eyes bright in the fire light. "You're not quite who I expected you to be."

"How so?" I asked.

"It's like... how can I put this gently?"

I waited.

"You told me you were a microbiologist, for example. I would never have guessed that. Somehow the world of medical science seems so far away from who you are now. Or at least from what I know of you, which isn't much, I know."

I nodded and added. "But isn't that true for all of us? I mean, the Shift changed everything."

"Yes, of course. But *that* industry though. The corporations and their patents, leaving the poor to die. The exploitation of sickness for profit. I mean the environmental impact alone..."

"I get that," I said, unsure if I had cut her off midstream or if she was finished. "But a lot of us benefited from the vaccines and medicines and still do."

"Of course. You're right. It just feels surreal somehow...I mean I worked in the stock market, for god's sake, I really can't talk."

I shrugged.

"How was it for you though?" she asked me. "Your work, I mean."

I thought for a moment. "I guess I just found it fascinating. I was obsessively clean as a kid and my immune system has never been great. For as long as I can remember, microbiology felt like something I could do, maybe even should do. And also, to be honest, I like things I can control and measure."

This wasn't the first time I was surprised by the words coming out of my mouth in Laguna's presence. "It felt nice to be doing work with results," I added. "And the money helped."

I often worried I was sharing too much with her, but at the same time, not quite enough to quench her curiosity. Conversation still felt like a precarious tight rope of a thing, but I could feel myself getting used to it, maybe even dependent on it. *I'll miss this when I go home.*

"Makes sense." Laguna looked down at the fire. "Still, it's just hard to imagine how we were ever part of that world now. Do you know what I mean?"

I shrugged again and noticed how gestures too were coming back to me. "My family was poor. I was the first to study beyond high school. I don't know... we had to do whatever we could to survive. And there were kind of no good choices, just slightly less bad ones."

"Capitalism," said Laguna. The weight of that memory lay heavy between us.

"If I'd had my way though," I said, trying to lighten the conversation, "I'd have been an ornithologist."

"Birds, really?"

I smiled. "I've always loved them."

"Me too."

"It's awful what happened."

"It is."

We fell quiet for a moment and watched the dwindling fire. Laguna stood up and added another log. It was clear she wanted to talk more. She looked at me and said softly, "I didn't know you grew up poor."

I nodded. "My parents both worked in a meat factory outside the city. And of course, the factories were the first hit during the pandemics—covid and later the superbugs. It was an industry drowning in anti-biotics. The whole thing imploded."

Laguna's expression changed but I didn't know how to interpret it. "They say that that's what caused it." She leaned forward. "The Shift, I mean."

"In what way?" I asked.

"Precarity?" Her voice became quieter. "As I heard the theory, a lot of the people who shifted were, or are, precarious in some way. Poor or trans or disabled or a hundred other things. One idea is that it was experiences of precarity that caused us to shift. Which is also why the non-shifted seem to mostly be a lot more privileged in general."

Laguna paused and looked thoughtful before concluding. "Or it was nature's last plea to prevent all-out destruction of the planet."

"All possible," I agreed diplomatically. "I guess we'll never know."

"But you understand the science of it?" she asked me. "Of the Shift?" Her eyes seemed especially bright.

"As much as any of us really understand it. Genetics wasn't my specialty," I admitted. "But I guess I have a handle on it. Horizontal gene transfer. The long-term effects of stress hormones. There were a lot of theories, I'm not sure anyone really knows for sure."

The fire was warm and bright and the new log was crackling.

"One thing I heard," Laguna began with a hint of insecurity, "is that it was a virus of some kind. That brought the new genetic codes."

I nodded then shrugged. "It was never conclusive—and now there's no way to know for sure—but yeah, that was the dominant hypothesis as I heard it too."

"It's weird," Laguna said thoughtfully. "That a virus could be useful to our survival."

"I don't know. In some ways, humans and viruses have been interwoven forever." I poked the fire with a stick then continued. "For example, around eight per cent of our genes comes from ancient viruses. They've been integrating themselves into vertebrate genomes for more than four hundred and fifty million years and a few are even essential to our survival. They've played a big part in us having placentas for example."

"I don't follow."

I paused. "I just mean that viruses and retroviruses are an integral part of our DNA. There's no part of us that hasn't been affected by them at some point. So in a way, it's nothing new."

"Okay, that's interesting though." Laguna's voice was enthusiastic. "So a new virus brought the Shift into our genes—and we changed—all in the same generation. Is that the idea?"

"More or less. It wouldn't be so strange really. There is this idea that evolution and natural selection are all about sexual reproduction and that changes are only passed down vertically between generations—so, from parents to offspring."

"Isn't that how it works?"

"Partially. But reproduction sex and inheritance through generations as the *only* mode of evolution is kind of an old-fashioned idea. There's a lot more to it in reality."

I wondered if I was information dumping—it wouldn't have been the first time I had gone off on a tangent and shared all the information I knew on a subject even after the other person had stopped listening. But Laguna's face showed surprise and curiosity. I continued.

"Evolution is a lot more complicated—and interesting—than a lot of us realise. Horizontal gene transfer is common, for example."

"What's that?"

"I guess you've heard about how bacteria often develop drug resistance by passing each other genes."

"Sure. That was where the superbug plagues came from."

"Right. And in that case, the genes for drug resistance aren't inherited, they're shared horizontally."

"Okay."

"And, though it's rarer, even some vertebrates have given each other DNA as well. For example, one species of fish gave another a gene for a kind of anti-freeze protein which was useful as they both live in very cold places. Potentially hundreds of human genes arrived this way. In a way, horizontal transfer is a fundamental driver of evolution. Particularly in the case of symbiogenesis."

"Symbio—"

"—genesis," I said. I took a breath while I thought how to explain it. "Our cells have power banks called mitochondria—"

"I remember those from school, I think."

"Right. And way back, mitochondria used to be bacteria who lived independently. So at some point our ancestors absorbed them, they became a part of us, and we gained their ability to get energy from respiration." I was almost out of breath. The words seemed like they were spilling out of me. "I think of it as a kind of queer theory for biology. Evolution often happens in a horizontal, non-linear, boundary-breaking way."

"That's fascinating." Laguna leaned in.

"The strange thing though," I continued, "is how all these changes happened within our lifetime. Even horizontally acquired changes need to make their way through a population. I actually heard a few interesting theories about that—"

Suddenly Laguna stretched her arms theatrically to the sky and yawned. She didn't look tired, and it was still early for us.

"Do you want to sleep in my bed tonight?"

She asked it so casually. I stared, and my brain struggled to keep up. Life has a way of moving suddenly too fast sometimes.

"Brook?" she asked after a moment of silence.

I blinked and breathed and said, "Not yet, if that's okay?"

"Of course, love," she replied, and my heart jumped a little. "More than okay."

"I mean, I want to." I blinked again. I wasn't entirely in control of my mouth.

She replied with one of her world-changing smiles and I took a moment to think.

"I wonder if—" I paused.

Her eyes asked me to continue.

"Could we *snuggle* maybe?" It was a strange word, but it fit perfectly with the image in my head.

She leaned forward again in such a subtle way that I don't think she even knew it happened.

"My place or yours?"

before

I'm not usually a spontaneous person but after I began to live by myself, casually hooking up with strangers became a regular part of my life. My new flat was on the eighth floor—no lift of course—and the lab was an hour's walk away. Resting between the journey back from work and the climb up to my place had become a daily ritual. My building had its own bar, one of several spilling out onto the square. I sat down and ordered fries and the cheapest beer on the menu, as I did every other day.

Even with a steady job, the paperwork needed to get a housing contract by myself had made it impossible and I ended up in a precarious sublet. The friend of my colleague had gone off to Peru on some ayahuasca trip and left her flat with my colleague while she was away. The friend seemed to have disappeared off the map and when my workmate moved in with her boyfriend, she said I could stay at the flat but would need to vacate quickly if the friend ever turned up. I have no idea how long it takes to find enlightenment in the rainforest, but I hoped it would take a while.

It wasn't a great situation, or even a particularly nice place, but it was cheap. And at least I only had to do my own laundry now. No more picking up Adam's socks or cleaning his ashtrays. No more fights on the balcony or listening to his porn at four in the morning.

I tried to comfort myself with these thoughts, but in fact, I'd have given anything to take a walk with Adam. Or cuddle together on the sofa.

Even sitting outside, the air was close and humid. The fries took a while to arrive, I drank my beer too fast, and I was feeling light-headed. A fashionably dressed, apparently straight, couple at the next table were being touchy with each other. They showed each other their phones and giggled at whatever they saw there. They rubbed each other's legs, and they kept glancing over at my table.

At first, I assumed they were making fun of me. With half the staff off sick, I was pulling extra shifts. It was two weeks since I'd had a day off and I'm sure I looked exhausted, sick, or both.

But I watched them a bit more closely. The glances they were giving me were telling me something else. They weren't mocking me, they were *interested*. In what, I couldn't be sure, but I had definitely caught their attention.

Abruptly, they stood and dragged their chairs over to my table. The guy asked, "Can we buy you another drink?" I felt like I should have been offended at the couple's audacity, but I was curious and, honestly, into it. I let them buy me a beer, and three more, before I invited them up to my place. I warned them about the stairs, and they laughed. They went to the gym together four times a week; they would survive. I didn't even know there were still gyms.

When we arrived, I opened the windows of the living room-bedroom to let some air in. The couple made themselves comfortable on the sofa-bed and continued touching each other. I meant to go to the kitchen and bring some wine. Or at least to go to the bathroom to freshen up. Instead, they pulled me in, and we started making out, the three of us.

The couple had a feral wildness to their affections, and seemed to share my feeling that there was nothing to lose at the end of the world. That's a powerful combination for having a good time.

But I soon began to feel like a tourist. There were confusing glances and raised eyebrows. He broke off a kiss to whisper something in her ear. She nodded and smiled. I was on the outside looking in.

The kissing was hot—and I've always loved that sensation of losing myself in multiple mouths—but I was becoming distracted by all the over-information and weird dynamics they had brought into my home. They both came, loudly. I didn't.

I headed to the kitchen to open a bottle of wine. Even if it was over, a drink would be good. After some mumbling and giggling from the other side of the wall, the couple found me there. It was not over.

After a few minutes of simultaneous kisses on my neck and my wrist, we ended up having sex on the kitchen counter. I was in the middle and this time I came hard. Two glasses and one of my favourite plates got smashed. They offered me money to cover the breakages and I wasn't too ashamed to take it.

The afternoon ended sooner than I expected. They both left me with lingering kisses goodbye, but no numbers were exchanged. At that time, no-one planned much beyond the next week; we all lived in the moment. I waited a few minutes then leaned out the window to watch them as they left the building below. They held hands as they stepped out into the drunken crowds of people gathering in the square. They never looked up.

I sat in an uncomfortable wooden chair watching the clouds get darker, my heart aching with a confusing sense of loss. The moon was nowhere to be seen and I went to sleep horny and exhausted.

The dappled light of the tent moved over my eyes, teasing me back to consciousness. I was immersed in the sounds of the village.

I stretched my arms up and bent over to one side and then the other. Gingerly, I moved my foot and…nothing. No pain shooting up through my ankle. Not even that weird crunching sensation that had become almost familiar. I sat up and placed both feet on the ground. *Still okay.* I stood, holding on to the side of the tent and kept my weight all on the left foot just in case. My weight shifted to the right. I took a step. It all felt fine!

I was elated to have my mobility back and decided in that moment that this day would be my last in the village. I had waited too long already to return home. Who knew what a mess the storm might have left behind? I had things to repair, a home to tidy. I wouldn't have to speak to another person for three weeks, minimum, especially if Laguna agreed to let me take some supplies. I was free!

I sat back down. *Laguna.*

The physical contact of the night before had been too intense for me. Or maybe just intense enough. As I sat on the bed where it had all happened, watching shadows on the tent wall, I was pulled into a trance of memory.

I felt again the rhythm of her breathing and her abdomen pushed against my lower back. Her finger tracing a tiny journey across my upper arm, a gentle accompaniment to a story told, sending shivers down my spine. I remembered her smell—so much more complex with proximity—and how she had talked about her grandmother who loved animals and had spent time on an island in Japan, overpopulated by rabbits. I had only half followed her words as I lay enchanted by her voice. I had felt more in my body, tense and excited and panicked as it was, than I had in a long time.

Without me saying a word, Laguna had known when to leave. She had sat up on my bed and barely able to see in the darkness, I knew she had smiled at me.

"Dream with the river creatures, my love," she had whispered softly and as she had left the tent I had pondered for a moment on this curious expression. Was it something from her native language or a Sasu term I'd never heard before? We had shifted in different bioregions, there was no reason to assume we even shared a vocabulary.

But I realised in that moment, still half-awake, that I *had* dreamed of water creatures that night. Tiny insects hidden in the reeds. Silver-sided fish breaching to escape a predator. And dark, fluffy chicks born on a floating platform of weeds and twigs.

I looked over the bed we had shared so briefly and turned to run my fingers over the sheet. Would she be okay with me leaving? Had the night before changed something? Was I even still *allowed* to leave, to go back to my own life, or had we crossed some kind of line? What would she expect from me now?

We had held each other for less than an hour, but intimacy doesn't recognise time. I had no idea what any of it was supposed to mean.

I tested my foot again. Perfect. I stood and walked over to the entrance, giving my walking stick a grateful glance as I went. I unzipped the door and stepped out into the morning. It was time to find out.

* * *

My ascension into the trees was clumsy and embarrassing and I was glad that no-one was around to see it. It helped that I had chosen a ladder at the edge of the village where people rarely went.

I have only a vague memory of climbing a tree before that day. I was a child, full of innocence and courage and in that parallel universe of youth, swinging, climbing, even sleeping up in a tree was something fun and exciting. This was nothing like that.

I had seen some of the villagers ascending on ropes using harnesses and karabiners. I had no equipment, and I wasn't in the mood to ask for any. I chose a rope ladder, and I was no more than two metres off the ground when it started swaying wildly from side to side. The 'rungs' were just thick sticks tied into the rope. They were slippery and rotated in their knots when I stood on them. I looked up briefly at the underside of the platform above me. The ladder was attached to a hole cut into the floor. It all seemed impossibly far away.

But I began to understand. I learned where to place my feet so that the rungs didn't shift as much and the swinging became less intense as I compensated by moving my weight—just a bit, I discovered, not too much.

I pushed up finally through the hole, threw myself dramatically onto the platform and rested on my back catching my breath. In my mind was the image of a seal emerging exhausted from a hole in ice. Well at least it wasn't ice. I looked around. In fact, it was magnificent.

Lining the platform floors, leaving plenty of space for people to make their way, raised beds overflowed with squashes and beans. The sides of the platforms were three long slats acting as walls, windbreaks and handrails. I stood up and placed my hands on the wooden rail. Between climbing vines and cascading flowers, the polished wood glowed red and brown in the morning light.

All around me, connected by platforms and rope bridges, small huts nestled amongst the trees. Lines of laundry swung in the breeze. I caught hints of pine and eucalyptus and inhaled deeply as I gripped the side of the platform. I knew then that this settlement was inseparable from the habitat it belonged to. The village was as much a part of the forest as the leaves and branches interspersed through the wooden structures.

I wanted to push on and find Laguna. We needed to talk about the night before. I needed to know where things stood with us. And yet I wasn't ready to pull my eyes away from the landscape.

I was facing south, the sun rising to my left. The winding river and the marsh spread out before me for kilometres, still covered in shadow and patches of fog. Beyond, a wavy line of bays and cliffs drew the end of the land and the beginning of the ocean. Home.

My eyes didn't dare to linger. I turned and crossed the platform. A broken carpet of forest stretched north, humming with life. At the horizon, mountains marked a dramatic end to our ecosystem and river basin.

I turned to the left, to take in the straight lines that only civilisation could have created. The windows of the old airport sparkled in morning red and even from afar I could see that the runway was slick with oil, the ground interrupted by the immense cracks left by seismic tremors.

My mind began to wander inevitably to earthquakes and how they arrived suddenly in our landscape. To the first I had ever experienced, and to the sheer terror of that day.

before

On the morning of the big demonstration, people filled the streets, and I was caught up in the moment. I marched despite my misgivings, and I chanted against poverty.

I don't think anyone was listening. Surely the people with the power to change things were the same people causing the problems. I figured that they had no interest in resolving them—no matter how many of us gathered or how loud we screamed. And yet I shouted as if my life depended on it. It was only my second demonstration and it was already bigger than anything I could have imagined.

In half a year, the country had been through five governments and demonstrations like this had become common place. The demands for whoever was in power at the time—and the corporations that ruled without pause—to provide the essentials of living to the population had become louder and more visible by the week.

I had also read online that some groups were already giving up on this culture of demanding change. They chose instead to create it for themselves by squatting land, growing food, building autonomous schools. And others chose to bring the fight to the doorsteps of the super-rich: some of the ultimate architects of all this suffering.

For now, I had chosen the path of least resistance. If five hundred thousand people could walk from A to B, I probably could too. Even if it wasn't clear to me yet what my role was or what was expected of me, I could at least be a part of something symbolic. Even with all my reservations it felt good, empowering maybe, to be doing something at last.

I hadn't planned to join though. I had heard the noise from outside my flat when I woke up. It was always loud in my home due to the poorly installed windows, but this was another level. I had woken up in a sweat, bathed in screams and whistles and chants. Nothing in the world would have gotten me back to sleep so I got dressed and joined in without even thinking about breakfast. In retrospect, I think I was already changing. Joining a demonstration of thousands? I was living someone else's life.

We had walked ten blocks when the ground beneath us began to shake.

With so much noise and so many angry footsteps, I barely noticed at first. And for a moment it felt like *we* were the ones creating the tremors—literal movement building or something. But soon it was undeniable. Buildings were swaying and flowerpots rained down from balconies. Panicked and confused, the crowd stampeded.

Barely three metres from where I was standing, a piece of roof smashed into the pavement. I separated from the group and ran down the widest boulevard I could find, out across the park, back home.

In front of my building, shaking and panting, I stood for a good ten minutes. The street was full of people, every one of them looking as terrified as me. The tremors subsided and when our building showed no signs of collapse, we went back inside. I climbed the stairs to my apartment and curled up under a blanket. It would have done nothing to protect me, but sometimes symbols are all we have.

I later learned that the tremors had already been happening for months. For a while they were barely a whisper, only noticed by geologists and their highly sensitive equipment. Considering the political situation—and the cause of the tremors—they were kept a guarded secret for as long as possible.

Scrolling on my phone for hours, I found a piece in a mainstream paper that discussed the quake. Our area wasn't normally seismically active—this part I knew—but capitalism, caught in its death grip, had been expanding fracking across the region. The land had been cracked open, new oil wells had been opened up all across the country and now we had earthquakes where before there were none.

And they were just starting.

I pulled my eyes away from the cracked airport and shook my head. The past sometimes felt too painful to recall, but also impossible to forget. I remembered then why I was up in the tree. I was searching for Laguna. *We need to talk.*

I walked to the end of the platform and tentatively stepped out onto the rope bridge. It was simple enough; one rope for my feet, one rope on either side for each hand. A net loosely enveloped the whole structure. The bridge was sturdier than I expected and for a moment, I had the sense of being in an adventure playground and had to remind myself that this was someone's home.

I paused midway and my mind wondered. I could see how building high was a practical solution, living in a marsh prone to storm flooding. I also knew, because I'd been living in one, that not all the homes were safe and high and not all the residents of the village were able to get up here if there was a flood or other danger. Who got to live here and who didn't? As I completed the bridge and stepped onto another blissfully solid platform, I realised I was getting more curious about the village. *How did all this get built?*

I briefly considered asking Laguna then shook my head.

I don't need all the answers, I told myself, *I'm leaving today.* And I had my own business to worry about.

Laguna's hut was at the end of the platform and her door was as beautifully crafted as any of the other structures up there. If anything, hers was more heavily covered in flowers, beans, and squashes. I knew it was her place because she had pointed it out to me from below one time and as we know, I'm weirdly good at remembering where things are.

I inhaled and knocked on the door and for the first time realised that she hadn't explicitly invited me and maybe I should have checked. My body tingled. Apprehension? Excitement?

No-one answered.

I knocked again, slightly harder and the door squeaked open. It felt like a transgression of boundaries, but before I could even engage with the thought, my feet were moving. I stood inside Laguna's home.

* * *

The change in light, from bright, unfiltered, morning rays to subdued red on wood was dramatic. The sudden hush of the protecting walls made me realise just how much noise there had been outside—the wind and raven-calls and bee-hums that I had been filtering out without knowing.

And the still air inside held so many smells of Laguna's life that I had to pull them apart to be able to tend to each one. There was warm chamomile and earthy nettle—bouquets of herbs hung drying in every corner of the room. There was the yeasty aroma of transition bubbling up from mysterious jars of fermentation on shelves. Untidy piles of books were clouded with dust and desiccation. Laguna's scent hung over every surface. Clothes dangled from a wire pulled tight between two hooks and her underwear was littered over the single armchair.

A black and white lizard scuttled across the windowsill and her 'tik-tik-tik-tik' sound was a warning to my body.

Enough. This was too much intimacy with no invitation. The room expelled me then as surely as a physical force pushing me back outside onto the platform.

And as I stood back out in the sunlight, I heard Laguna's voice.

It was distant and I could tell that she wasn't talking to me. I walked towards it, to the edge of the platform, and leaned out over the safety barrier. I saw perhaps the entire village gathered in a huge circle. Laguna sat among them; her silhouette now as familiar to me as my own shadow. Even from up high, I could see her hands moving as she talked.

That's where I need to be.

What happened next was surprising and entirely without justification.

I can only imagine that I wasn't in control of my decision-making when I crossed another platform that took me to the entrance of the green water slide. Its plastic mouth was inviting in a way I knew it shouldn't be. I could think of a hundred ways I might injure myself going down, and without water running through it, would I even go anywhere or just get stuck halfway? It had been built for a waterpark, somewhere with lifeguards and chlorinated water and proper attachments to the wall and electricity for the red and green lights that were still attached but quite dead. In no sensible universe should I have launched myself down that thing.

But it *was* wonderful. The twists, the echoes of my own surprised sounds coming back to me as I hurtled through a tunnel of green-filtered light. I thrilled to the heart-clenching drop as I launched weightlessly into fresh air and crashed down into the river water.

As I pulled myself out onto the riverbank—still fully clothed and without even a towel to dry myself with—thoughts flooded back into my mind.

Of how life could have been different. Of everything that was possible, just one microscopic step away in another universe. Of potential, and choices, and gravity.

I stood...and pushed it away. It was too late. The direction of my life was already established, and I didn't need anything else. Sometimes what already is, has to be enough. I turned and made my way towards the circle of humans that stood between me and my home.

* * *

In the village circle, a few people glanced over as I arrived, but as usual, they discretely looked away. I still couldn't tell if it was judgment for who I was and what I had done to Laguna, or if they were just naturally wary of strangers. Both would make sense. I also had the good grace to know that I couldn't read minds, and sometimes it wasn't helpful to try.

I found an empty spot on the grass and sat down cross-legged. I carefully touched my ankle and it still felt fine. A village member was speaking; someone I'd never talked to.

That in itself wasn't strange as, besides Laguna, I'd probably spoken to less than four villagers and even those were short, polite exchanges. But I found it odd that I had never at least noticed this person. Although everyone sat in a circle—because we're all equal, no matter who's speaking, Laguna had explained to me—I had the sense that they could have been up on a stage delivering a lecture. Their presence was electric.

"Something else that's interesting about Sasu, at least our little part of it—", they were saying, their eyes sparkling, "—is that it's so flexible. It's really designed to be co-created as a language by those who live inside it. The word chee' for example. It just means 'thing' but add almost anything to it and you have a new word. Can anyone give me an example?"

One person, the older baker whose name I still hadn't learned, said "Fire-chee'."

Oven, I translated in my head.

The storyteller nodded.

"Knot-chee'," said one of the kids.

Rope.

And so it went on. Sit-chee'. Sleep-chee'. Everyone seemed to have their own way of pronouncing the glottal stop at the end of the words.

One person, who might have been in their early twenties, suggested pleasure-chee', which I'd never heard before, but I could guess a few translations.

The storyteller smiled. "See how it allows us to be creative? It's emergent. As each speaker uses Sasu, they adapt it just a little to reach their goals. All languages do this, but what makes a slang like Sasu different is that it was created precisely for this reason—to express our changing needs and to bring us better into relationship with our other-people family."

The baker put up her hand.

"Go ahead," said the storyteller. "This isn't school."

"Right," she said. "I have a question. You call Sasu a slang, but I was told it was a language and now that I'm saying it, I'm not even sure what the difference is."

"Officially, people call it a cant slang," the storyteller explained. "—communication designed for sharing secrets among a small community. There have been other cant slangs like this: Hijra Farsi, Polari, Kochemer Loshn—Sasu even incorporated some of their vocabulary. In these cases, sometimes the in-group was sex workers or criminals or queer or trans people, anyone who needed to keep secrets from the outside world. In the case of Sasu, we've never been quite sure who the in-group is."

"But surely," said the baker, "Sasu developed around the same time as the Shift. So isn't the in-group as you call it, us, the shifted?"

"It does seem that Sasu speaks to our new shifted experiences. But by now it's probably also been adopted by the non-shifted, or the Fittest." The storyteller whispered the words. "Or whatever they call themselves now. I'm honestly not sure."

The mention of the Fittest brought an awkward silence to the group and I felt myself tensing. Talking about those who hadn't realigned with us had become something of a taboo—we all knew the horror stories.

The storyteller brought us back out of it gracefully. "So yes, Sasu is sometimes a slang—derived from various languages, loaning new grammatical functions and useful terms. And in a few places, Sasu is its own full language. This flexibility is part of what allowed it to enter our hearts and spread so quickly."

I listened without any interrupting thoughts. Some people have such enthusiasm for their subject that you can't help being pulled in when they talk about it. The storyteller paused to take a sip of water then looked around the circle making gentle eye contact with the others.

"Which brings us of course to one of my favourite stories—the origins of Sasu."

There was the subtlest of movements throughout the group. Some kind of ease, or maybe a dropping into something. People got ready to hear a story.

before

Alone, in my apartment, I sat by the window drinking limeflower tea. The cup was warm in my hands, the flavour was like summer sun on dry grass. I relaxed into the sofa with a sigh. The city could be exhausting. Sometimes it felt like I was under constant observation, and it was a relief to be inside at the weekend where no-one could see or judge me. *There should be a word for that feeling,* I mused, as I watched clouds pass by.

In retrospect, I'm not sure the eighth floor of an apartment building was a great place to be the day after an earthquake. And yet, alone in my space, on my lumpy sofa-bed by the window, I felt safer than anywhere else I could be. The outside world was full of people and sometimes people are just too difficult.

Or human-people at least, I thought to myself as I watched a raucous quarrel of sparrows visiting the plastic bird feeder I had attached to the rail of the balcony.

They hopped between pots of herbs and climbed over each other to get the best spots on the feeder. They made quick alliances and even quicker conflicts and somehow, they all got enough to eat. More sparrows came, including fluffy fledglings still fed by their parents, and others left to wherever sparrows go when we're not watching them.

Although I wasn't used to thinking in that way, there was suddenly no doubt in my mind that these were also people. *Sparrow-people, we could say,* although it sounded strange for me to put the words together like that. More-than-human people. Other-people. I felt like my language wasn't enough to express the kinship I felt in that moment for the fuzzy, chirping visitors at my window. Refilling their feeder and drinking tea with them, Saturday passed in a blissful, reflective blur. Loneliness didn't even occur to me.

It was Sunday evening when I first noticed that something was wrong with the sparrows. A young female, who I recognised, sat on the balcony rail, far away from the others. Even through the window glass I could see she was trembling. I heard her cough once: a small but terrible sound. Then with startling abruptness, she collapsed into a pot of thyme. She lay there motionless. I stood and reached for the door handle, but another sparrow fell. And then a third.

I went to the bathroom and put on latex gloves. By the time I returned, there were ten or more, some twitching on the balcony floor, the others deathly still. I opened the door and carefully picked up the young female. I had known her for most of her life, her parents had brought her to the feeder just days after she fledged. And now her body lay cold in my hands. The flu had arrived in the city and the devastation was just beginning.

<h1 style="text-align:center">after</h1>

Every good tale starts with an origin story and Sasu is no different."
The villagers leaned in, already enthralled. The storyteller's bare feet were planted on the ground as if drawing the stories up from the soil itself.

"Even to this day, we don't really know where Sasu came from," they continued. "Some say, the other-people themselves taught us the first words, less than a decade ago, calling us back into kinship with them. Some have suggested that it emerged from our DNA as we shifted. Our genes, our bodies, and our minds transitioned in response to the end of everything and along with that shift came a new form of expression."

I fiddled with my fingers. I had heard this argument before but had never been convinced. *There's no evidence that language can*—I paused mid-thought and swallowed. I decided not to analyse. This was a story and sometimes stories need their own space to grow.

"For me, Sasu began during the pandemics with a single human-person, alone at home. It's said that she was a woman, but I've heard others suggest man, or neither of those. Or both. Some say it was a group of friends sat around in a circle, like we are today, with meeting notes and word-books, and big plans. But for me, she was alone. As her protection-chee'—her immune system—was compromised, she wasn't able to leave her home for several years. Wave after wave of plagues filled the streets around her and she didn't see many people except the occasional nurse or someone bringing her supplies."

"She was by herself, but a tree stood outside her window—some say a poplar, some say a willow—and that single tree, changing through the seasons, was her lifeline. It began with just a few words. 'Su' to describe the sound of the morning wind in the branches, which became the word for all conversation and gave us Sasu, people-language. 'Chitt' for the tense sounds of a territorial sparrow, that became the verb for negotiation and compromise. The alarm sound of a blackbird gave us 'seep', our word for danger. And in this way, Sasu began to grow inside her."

I looked briefly around the circle. No-one moved, even the children sat still, enraptured. I couldn't help but respond internally to the story. My protection-chee' was also weak. I had spent plenty of time alone at home. But while this mythical person, if she had ever existed, had created an entire animist slang during her isolation, I had achieved next-to-nothing in my life.

I recognise that that probably wasn't completely true, or particularly fair to myself.

I know that we marginalised people don't need to produce work, or culture, or even social change to be deserving of love. I know all that, but still those were the thoughts I was sitting with in that moment.

The storyteller continued: "One day, the creator of Sasu, or the translator-of-the-trees as she's also called, began to teach the new way of communicating to others. Words themselves were easy enough, people have been picking up new vocabularies forever and as I mentioned, some of the new words and phrases were imported and adapted from other languages and slangs. But the grammar took more effort. One thing that was difficult to grasp for those with certain first languages were the animate pronouns."

"In pre-shift English for example, only a few precious beings were usually considered worthy of being called he, she, they or who. A human child was considered animate enough to be a 'he' or 'she', but a pigeon was invariably called 'it'. A dog or cat was also an 'it', unless they lived in a house, then they became close enough to earn an animate gender and their human companions would be very offended if you called their precious poodle, 'it'."

There was light laughter around the circle.

"When we describe a river as 'it', the river seems more like a dead and unchanging object, a thing that can be blocked or diverted; a resource to be exploited. When we say the 'river who I crossed this morning', we are drawn into a deeper connection with an ever-changing presence. And in pure Sasu, as some of you know, there are several ways to show how animate a noun is. Not surprisingly, many Indigenous languages have similar ways of talking about the land and that's almost certainly the source of some of the grammar in Sasu. Human-people can't possibly survive somewhere for tens of thousands of years if the land is something dead you can destroy instead of a living presence with whom you can engage."

The story continued for a while longer, but my attention drifted. I got lost in thoughts of the mass extinction of Indigenous languages. Of the importance of respect. And of waves and sand and home and the Sasu words to express those actions and beings.

before

In my apartment, I sat motionless on the floor. My brain and body felt numb as I took in another news broadcast. Bird flu was back: a new subtype, more pathogenic than ever, was tearing through bird populations and the poultry industry. It was all happening again.

It wasn't limited to the sparrows who I had carefully collected from my balcony, wearing gloves and a mask, and buried in the park. It was the hooded crows and the kingfishers too, the blackbirds, and the tufted ducks. The virus had ended its hiatus and our window of opportunity was closed. Once again, our short memories meant death.

Now, according to the enthusiastic news anchor who spoke breathlessly and gripped the blank papers in front of her, avian flu was back with more force than ever. The new subtype seemed unstoppable, enhanced biosecurity showed no effect, and there was no time to cull because whole factory populations of ducks, turkeys and chickens were dead within hours. In just a few weeks, parts of the global poultry industry were already showing signs of collapse.

The local news came on, and still I sat there, bathed in the soporific blue light of the TV. In the past week, several people in my area had been mugged after buying the last cartons of eggs in the supermarket. I recognised the street, only two blocks from my home. The night before, a woman had been knifed to death over a roast chicken. And as the economy continued to implode, the food riots were spreading like fire.

I stood and physically brushed myself off as though the horrifying news was just settled dust that could be made to go away. I walked over to the balcony door and saw that a tiny blue tit lay twitching in a pot of basil. I couldn't bring myself to feel the loss.

I stepped over to the coffee table and picked up a flyer I had been given during the ill-fated demonstration the week before. In a dramatic font, it read:

Tired of fighting to be heard? Ready to come together and find solutions? Join our weekly planning meetings at the village hall, Tuesdays at 6pm. Together we will make it through this crisis.

There was a website, a code, and several social media handles, but I was already convinced. If the demonstration had felt somewhat empowering, then being part of planning the next one, or any of the neighbourhood initiatives listed on the flyer, might be even better. I could go straight to the meeting the next day from work.

It had to be better than another evening alone watching the news.

after

The storyteller ended their tale of Sasu's origins softly. There was no abrupt ending, no take-away lesson, they simply faded us back into the moment and fell quiet to allow the humming of bees and the scents of river and grass to envelope us. I felt closer to the others in the village than before I sat down. We had been part of this shared experience.

After a few moments of quiet I moved my weight uncomfortably. I still needed to speak to Laguna, and I didn't want to wait anymore. Across the circle, she sat perfectly still, her hands in her lap, her eyes closed. A metallic blue damselfly rested on her knee, their tiny wings the darkest indigo beneath. This was a moment that wasn't ready to be disturbed. And it was a collective moment. Discussing the intimacy of the night before, telling her that I was ready to return home, that all felt private. I would need to find her alone after the gathering was over.

Then, as if to delay me even further, food arrived. Plates piled high with salad, bread, and steamed spinach fresh from the garden. My mouth was watering before my plate even arrived, passed hand to hand around our gentle circle.

before

I was hungry as I entered the village hall through the main entrance. I hadn't slept well the night before—unsurprising after the horror of the evening news—and work had been too busy to get lunch. Public transport was disrupted by demonstrations across town, so I had walked the four kilometres from the lab. When I arrived, the hall was already full.

I took a seat on a plastic folding chair. It felt fragile enough that it might fall apart if I moved around too much. I felt the same way and remained perfectly still.

There was a stage, podium, and a pile of cables at the back of the room, but the fifty or so people were gathered in a big circle, facing each other—which felt appropriate. My first impressions of those present were confusing. Faded black hoodies were abundant. Jeans were torn or stained. I didn't see a single pair of shoes that weren't scuffed, muddy or faded.

Somehow it made me suspicious. I looked at my own trainers and jeans, imperfect and out of fashion, but as clean and neat as I could maintain them.

Class is complex. I know this, deep down. It is an embodied experience and not one I discuss lightly. But class is what I was thinking about in that room. In my family we'd always prioritised dressing as well as we could. When you're poor, you don't want anyone to know you're poor. That isn't everyone's experience and I'm not saying it's good. Having such high standards is a lot of pressure, sometimes it's impossible, and I often found it annoying. But it's absolutely something that my parents had instilled in me from a young age.

In contrast, here were people who seemed proud to look like they didn't have a washing machine or money for new shoes. Honestly, although I know this makes me sound like a reverse snob or something, the elective-scruffiness bothered me, and I wasn't convinced by their accents either.

The thing that really pushed me out of the moment though, was the lack of food.

I hadn't thought of bringing anything to eat. Surely everyone in a meeting like this would be in the same situation as me—or probably much worse. Surely someone would have planned a meal. I had money in my pocket to contribute. I was even ready to go out and bring some food for us if needs be. But the meeting started abruptly with no logistics, no introductions, and no consideration for the day we might be coming from.

Within half an hour, my stomach was rumbling, and I was distracted. After two hours—when we were finally granted a 'quick one-minute break'—I left and didn't return.

after

As I ate my meal with the villagers, I fell deeply into my senses. Perhaps it was the story we had been told that brought me into the moment, perhaps the food was so fresh and flavourful, it pulled me in through its own force. I tasted every bite, every acid crunch of tomato between my teeth, the oregano leaves still plump with life, slightly astringent on my tongue. The fermented community of bread and the iron fullness of steamed leaves. And the dazzling blue of the little damselfly who still sat on Laguna's knee as she ate.

There was so much to do, so much to discuss. But the moment refused to let me go. I simply ate.

I wish spaces like the village could take credit for having gotten more inclusive with food and meetings, but I have a feeling that this was just one more manifestation of the Imperative pushing us—inspiring us—to be kinder to each other. For the most part we noticed when someone who should be present, wasn't. We noticed when someone was being silenced, excluded, or hurt. And we showed up for each other's needs— needs as basic as eating. I wish we could have learned that without the world going to hell, but here we are.

As the plates were collected, I realised I had no idea who was doing all the kitchen work. I had met the bread person, but there must be a whole team harvesting, cooking, cleaning. *Invisible work*, I noticed. *It's so easy to forget, even for people like me.* I decided then to ask Laguna. Maybe I could do a shift in the kitchen before I left.

Almost as if she knew that I was thinking of her, Laguna cleared her throat and all heads turned in her direction.

"That was amazing, thank you so much." She made eye contact with a few individuals, and they nodded in acknowledgement. "I have one thing I'd like to discuss before the food-sleep kicks in. It should take less than twenty minutes and it's about a plan that some of you know we've been working on for a few weeks."

There were nods and murmurs around the group.

"Now more than ever, we desperately need to finish the fence. We can't risk another visit from the night-dogs. We lost three chickens last time, and we need to find a solution."

Laguna caught the eye of a young person who I imagined might be responsible for the chickens. They looked sad and determined in equal measure.

"A group of us will head to the airport this afternoon. We found construction materials there before and we need more to complete the fence. But it's dangerous. The building has been damaged by quakes. It's been a while since we've had tremors so we should be safe enough, but please bear that in mind."

I thought about the cracks I had seen in the runway. Compared to this village of bending trees and flexible rope bridges, the airport seemed like a precarious construction from another age.

"It's also going to be a distance to get there over some rough land, so consider whether that kind of mobility is available to you." Laguna paused to allow her words to sink in and to give us a chance to consider our options. After a few minutes she asked softly, "Any volunteers?"

My hand went up without my conscious control.

before

As I stood outside the village hall, thinking about where I could get something to eat, a stranger came over and offered me a cigarette.

"No, I'm okay thanks", I mumbled, avoiding eye contact. After two hours of hearing men speak in a meeting, I wasn't in the mood to talk to anyone. And I had never smoked.

"You look like you need one though. I'm Cooper."

I looked up slowly and took in the details of this stranger. In a disconnected part of my brain, I realised that Cooper was handsome. Taller than me and unlike the posers inside, I remember thinking, he was well-dressed. His brown hair was short and combed. He had a local accent that was comforting to me.

"And you?"

"Brook," I replied. "I don't smoke, but thanks."

Cooper smiled and lit up a cigarette. The smoke drifted over me and for whatever reason, I didn't hate it.

"Sure?" he asked offering me the pack. "You really look like you need one."

In retrospect, that's a weird thing to say—twice—to someone you don't know. In the moment, I didn't notice. Whether it was my frustration with the meeting, my low blood sugar or just a sense of what's the worst that could happen, I took Cooper's cigarette.

I didn't even cough.

∗ ∗ ∗

The meeting break, and cigarette, were soon over but I didn't go back inside the village hall. My mouth was dry. I was slightly nauseous, so I leaned against the brick wall. My senses were overwhelmed by tobacco and the smell of Cooper's cologne.

The small talk lasted less time than the cigarette. He told me I was gorgeous, sexy. He leaned close and whispered some of the things he'd love for us to do together, experiments he wanted to try.

There was no doubt that I found him hot. Some part of me also wondered if this new stage of hooking up with strangers at bars and outside buildings was something I really wanted for my life. It happened anyway. Within twenty minutes of meeting him, I was in Cooper's bed covered in his sweat.

Somewhere in the middle of the night, we started sharing fantasies and our sex turned into playtime. I tied him up, he licked my toes. We did it in the shower, twice and he came over his own glass coffee table.

As morning light began to spill over our exhausted bodies, I realised that it had been a good twenty hours since I'd eaten anything substantial. Cooper must have heard my stomach rumbling—he jumped out of bed to cook breakfast, which he then laid out with serviettes and freshly squeezed orange juice on his generous balcony full of plants. We chewed quietly, watching as the sky became lighter. We squeezed in one more round of sex before I really had to get going.

I arrived late for work and my colleague gave my messy hair a judgemental glance as I passed by, making a beeline for my lab.

It was a particularly boring shift and I poked at my samples without paying much attention while I waited for the computers to catch up. In the sterile room that was generally designed to smell like nothing, I noticed the tobacco still lingering on my hair and skin despite several showers. It was overlaid with Cooper's absurdly expensive shampoo and just a hint of sex.

He had asked me to meet him again that night after work. When he told me where we were going, I agreed without hesitation.

after

Around two hours after our meal, equipped with an empty backpack and two litres of water, I set out with ten other villagers towards the airport.

I had a strange sense of internal conflict as two contradictory ideas both fought for dominance in my mind. I was meant to be leaving the village, yes, but in the *other* direction, *towards* home. Back to the beach and the crabs and my beautiful cave. And I was supposed to be alone. That was the plan and I always stick to my plans, which is part of the reason I enjoy making them.

I had spoken to Laguna briefly after the meeting but only to let her know that my ankle was better, and that I'd like to join the airport mission if I could be helpful. She seemed glad. I had wanted to talk more with her, to tell her my plans to return home, but the words got stuck in my throat and during that tiniest of delays, three other people came up to ask her questions.

The whole decision to join felt slightly unreal and I could easily blame the Imperative inspiring me to participate in a social activity, to help maintain a life-giving community. But that also felt like an easy excuse. Part of me wanted to give something back to these people who had helped me to heal over the last week and, in a way, had been sustaining my hermit lifestyle for years.

And when thoughts of home brought memories of crystal veins and flashes of lightning hitting the sea, I knew I was still wracked with guilt over what I had done. I needed to find a way to make amends. A trip for supplies was probably the least I could do.

The ground was flat and easy to navigate. Laguna walked ahead of me and after finishing a conversation with a villager, she slowed down and matched my pace.

"Thanks for coming along," she said brightly. "I'm glad your ankle is doing better."

"It's a lot better," I replied. "I even went up to your place to see you this morning."

Laguna looked surprised. "Really?"

"I wanted to talk with you about last night. Then I realised you were in the village circle, so I came back down to join you there."

"Do you still need to talk?"

"Yes, but it feels... private."

"Then let's pause for a while, we can catch up with the others."

And so we stopped and sat on a warm patch of rock surrounded by trees. I noticed the scent of pine needles, the rust-coloured lichens growing on the stone beneath us. I took a deep breath to steady myself, but the words tumbled out under their own power.

"So I don't know if you expect something from me now?" I blurted. "After last night, I mean. I know we just...snuggled...but I need to go home...erm, before tonight if possible." I inhaled. "The village is nice, you're nice. I'm very grateful for everything. And sorry for what I did. But I do need to go home, I can't stay here, I just...well yeah, okay, that's it."

Laguna looked away and seemed lost in thought. She took time to reply.

"Brook, I don't expect anything from you. When you're ready, of course you should go home." She turned her head back to me and made soft eye contact. "But I have one question—was it okay for you last night? Lying together in your bed? I know we checked, but you seem upset, and I'd like to know—did I do something that upset you?"

"I..." I paused to think. "It was good. I really liked it."

Laguna smiled. "Good. Me too."

"And...I dreamed of river creatures!"

"Amazing. I thought you might." Laguna got to her feet slowly. "Shall we go?"

Just a five-minute conversation and the tension that had sat with me the whole morning was dispersed. Laguna had power that enthralled and frightened me in equal parts. She helped me to my feet, and we pushed on towards the airport glittering on the horizon. The others were already halfway there.

before

Cooper and I arrived at the building an hour before closing. There was no queue, no sign of other visitors at all, and the guy at the front desk gave us a strange look.

Maybe he was confused why anyone would visit a museum when the world was burning. Or why two people, obviously on a date, would choose this of all places.

But Cooper had assured me we'd get in and we did.

The guy accepted our money and discretely put it in his pocket. He never touched the till, and I didn't blame him—no-one could be sure if their pay cheques would arrive anymore. We stepped into the hall, empty of people, and were greeted by the immense swooping neck of a sauropod.

after

Entering an abandoned airport was surreal to say the least. Not just because it had been such a long time since I'd taken a trip anywhere with other human-people, but also because there's something about the design of buildings like that that makes them seem as if they physically ache when they're empty.

The architecture is calling out for busyness, for the controlled chaos of crowds being directed from one point to another. The echoing check-in lounges and waiting halls gave me the strangest feeling of unease in my belly. None of this felt right.

I hadn't been in a lot of pre-Shift buildings recently. Spaces like my home or the village were fundamentally different from this monstrous industrial design. Every element chosen, every decision made since the Shift, was increasingly in consultation with the land.

Our new world was imperfect. Of course it was. The generations of my family before me were poor and transient, like me. We might not have experienced meaningful access to land since enclosure. So we were all improvising...a lot. This transition from industrial beings to becoming consciously part of nature again was completely new and yet incredibly ancient.

But for those of us who shifted, it became something like breathing—it just happened and nothing else would make sense. An airport building felt unimaginable until I was standing inside it.

As if the long, empty benches and scattered suitcases weren't surreal enough, the walls were lined with dinosaurs.

before

Cooper knew about my dinosaur obsession. The night before during a post-orgasmic lull, we had been propped up on pillows, drinking wine, and tangled in bedsheets and I'm really not sure how it came up. I'm aware that dinosaurs are a very odd thing to talk about on a first date. Especially a date that had been ninety-five percent sex and almost no talking. I was relieved that he didn't laugh at me or judge my geekiness. Instead, he jumped on it, said he had an idea for our second date that I was going to love.

As we walked through the hall alongside the twenty-metre-long skeleton, I knew he wasn't wrong.

I've always been into them. Escaping into magazines, online classes and my own Mesozoic fantasies as a kid had made everything more spacious. When life was difficult—which it usually was—I imagined the ground rumbling to the mountainous steps of sauropods, tiny *Procompsognathus* running around their feet and herds of *Iguanadons* migrating to water. Anything felt possible.

Cooper took my hand and led me around the exhibits.

"This is a *Brachiosaurus,*" he informed me and held my hand.

I smiled. It wasn't my first time at the museum and I knew, in fact, that this was a mislabelled *Giraffatitan*. In 2009 they had been recategorized to a new genus—the museum wasn't up to date, and apparently neither was Cooper. He'd probably learned the name from a movie or something. And only a few bones were actual fossils, most of the 'skeleton' was reconstruction.

"It's the longest sauropod ever discovered," he boasted as if he'd found the specimen himself.

Also untrue. An *Argentinosaurus* was ten metres longer at least. Cooper really wasn't that knowledgeable but seemed intent on impressing me with random facts about the displays we saw all around us. He wasn't even subtle about it. I caught him more than once reading an information panel before turning to tell me about the defensive strategies of the *Ankylosaurus* or how well preserved this particular *Scelidosaurus* was and—look there, I could see the stomach contents, how amazing!

It should have been annoying, but on Cooper I found it all charming. He was trying so hard, and I took it as a compliment. In all honesty, with his button-down shirt and his beige trousers he was giving off Palaeontology professor vibes and I was hot for it. We had the whole museum to ourselves and he seemed to be getting more attractive with each exhibit.

We went into a closed, dark room at the back of the museum. An *Archeopteryx* was on permanent display with constantly changing lights to highlight the delicate feathers and hollow bones. Cooper informed me that *Archeopteryx* was the first flying dinosaur and that they eventually became birds. Not really, but close enough.

We fucked in that room and my ass left a smear on the glass.

after

The airport was a flurry of cooing, flapping, and nesting pigeons. Avian dinosaurs.

A cavernous and sheltered building like this was a perfect place for them to breed and there were thousands flitting between their nests on windowsills, light fittings, and dark vending machines.

Pigeons are dinosaurs who developed flight. Like all modern birds, they are part of the only lineage that survived the mass extinction and went on to take over again in their noisy, infinitely adaptive way. I learned this when I was eleven: dinosaurs still ruled the earth and I had been watching them visiting my home-made bird feeder since I was an infant. They didn't just come from dinosaurs, they *are* dinosaurs, a fact that still makes my heart beat faster.

But they weren't the only ones in the airport.

I walked through the benches of the waiting lounge over to a display by the wall. My eyes landed on an explanatory panel, dark and cracked but still legible. As the panel informed me, the dusty items in the exhibit were bones, replicas of bones, and fanciful, colourful reconstructions of feathered dinosaurs on loan from China. I could hardly have been more excited.

Hand in hand, Cooper and I walked through another exhibit, *Euoplocephalus,* on a stage behind information panels and a rope. One of my favourites. I told Cooper how I wished I could get closer to inspect the palpebral bones and osteoderms.

"Just climb over the rope if you want to," he encouraged. "There's no-one here."

I've never been a rule-breaker, but I was almost tempted. Just then, I noticed the ticket guy lingering in a corner. Apparently, he was working security as well. Or he was just bored and wanted to watch.

Even Cooper wasn't that fearless. We walked briefly through the gift shop, but everything was more money than I wanted to spend and was mostly aimed at kids anyway. After a few minutes, Cooper took my hand and led me to the bathroom.

I stepped into the stall after him, got on my knees and began to blow him off. Cooper couldn't get enough. Even after knowing each other for just over a day, I knew exactly what he liked and had adapted my rhythm enough to give it to him. He was right on the edge and kept calling my name with increasing volume when suddenly there was a knock on the stall door. It was the ticket guy again, telling us it was time to leave. At least he sounded bored more than pissed off.

I was embarrassed but after zipping up his trousers, Cooper opened the door with what felt to me like exaggerated confidence. He gave the guy a wink and slipped him some coins. We went to pick up our coats.

The whole interaction felt a bit off. *What was that wink about?* I wasn't anyone's conquest.

I pushed the thought away and focused on the excitement of the night; the thrill of getting caught. And the burning attraction I couldn't deny. We left the museum and stepped out into the cool evening, hand in hand.

Turning the corner, Cooper paused, flashed me a grin and reached into his jacket. He produced a keyring and a plastic figure that was maybe meant to be an *Ankylosaur.* They still had the price tags on.

"I stole them for you."

As he handed me the toys, I realised in that moment that Cooper—still a virtual stranger—already knew enough about me to be dangerous.

after

Laguna watched as I stepped carefully over the guard rope to get closer to the display. At some point, the skeletons in the airport had been protected by glass, but the floor was now littered with dust-covered shards. I ran my finger over a skeleton embedded in stone. A *Microraptor,* according to the label. The streaks of pigeon faeces encrusting the fossil just made the experience even more resonant.

I heard Laguna arrive next to me, but my complete attention was focused on the fossilised tissues beneath my fingers. A hundred and twenty million years old, an inconceivable number. A flying dinosaur the size of a chicken, but one third of the weight—with no less than *four* wings. Two where we'd expect them and feathered legs for extra lift.

"Beautiful, right?" she said, her voice reaching through my reverie. "*Microraptor*?"

I looked up at her. "Yes. Did you read the sign?"

"I've been here before." She smiled at me. "And I've always loved dinosaurs."

I wasn't sure how to respond. I said: "*Microraptor* is really special. From what we can tell, they had glossy black feathers. Their pigment cells were stacked in layers so they might even have been iridescent."

"Like starlings."

"Like starlings."

For whatever reason my heart was beating too fast.

"They're really special," said Laguna softly. "Let's find the others?"

We stepped back over the rope, and I followed Laguna out of the hall.

* * *

We took so many turns through dark corridors that I doubted even *I'd* be able to find my own way out again. Although passengers had only ever seen a small part of the airport, the building ran for kilometres behind the scenes. It was a labyrinth of corporate offices, holding cells and confusing signage. To me, all of it felt like it belonged to an ancient era of history. Even if most of my life had been spent in that time.

I followed Laguna into what looked like a stock room of some kind. The villagers were lined up along the shelves, filling their backpacks with bags of peanuts, tiny cartons of UHT milk and precious rolls of toilet paper.

"All okay here?" Laguna asked the closest person who was balanced on a footstool pulling down a box of sanitary products. They nodded and smiled. "This will keep us going for a while."

Laguna politely returned the smile and led me through yet another door, this one with a green Fire Exit sign above it. We stepped out into the afternoon light, and I had to squint my eyes until they adjusted.

We were suddenly adrift on a sea of asphalt.

I gasped as my senses tried to take it in. The runway was crisscrossed with deep gashes. A few hundred metres away, I could see two colossal aeroplanes, the nose of one rammed into the side of the other. Suitcases were littered everywhere.

Although I had seen the airport many times from afar, the details up close were shocking. The air smelled of fuel and noxious chemicals. It was a scene of total devastation.

"I didn't know it was so bad," I said.

"Yes," Laguna replied and turned to the right.

We followed the outside of the building for another hundred metres until we arrived at an area piled high with all kinds of construction materials. She paused and put her hands on her hips to appraise the wooden slats, reels of barbed wire and electric cables.

"This should do nicely," she announced. "Is it okay if I leave you here to sort through this?"

I hesitated. I wasn't expecting to be left alone on this mission.

"I guess so?"

"Or not," she replied. "I know you mentioned you like organising things and I wanted to scout around the building and see if anyone's been here lately."

I looked again at the jumble of materials.

"Leave me to it," I said as I knelt, and began sifting through the treasure.

before

I sipped on my cocktail and watched Cooper watching me. The drink was so sweet it made my heart race, and I liked it.

Three nights after our date at the museum—the first time we were both free again—Cooper had invited me to a cute, but pricey café-bar near his house. I had wanted to drink on the terrace to enjoy the cool evening, but Cooper preferred privacy. We had our drinks at the back, in a corner behind the bar.

It took me two drinks to find the courage, but I finally managed to tell him. He was talking about cars or something and I just blurted it out.

"I'm trans, by the way. I don't know if you knew that."

His eyes widened slightly. I hoped it was my lack of conversation etiquette that had surprised him.

"I suspected," he said. He took a drink from his glass, placed it down heavily and wiped his mouth with the back of his hand. For whatever reason, he refused to drink from a straw and already our table was littered with wet straws, paper umbrellas and half-chewed orange slices. "It's all good."

I was relieved. Whatever assumptions he was making, it was better to get it out there.

But his response also left me unsettled. My gut physically reacted to the word 'suspect'. His 'all good' bothered me more than I cared to admit. *I wasn't asking permission.*

Maybe it was the rum that soothed my concerns. Maybe it was the way he ran his fingers around the edge of his glass and looked at me like I was a delicious treat. I leaned in and kissed him.

After our drinks, he suggested that I sleep over again. I had an early start the next day and politely refused. The kiss that he gave me as we parted ways outside the bar was demanding and hungry.

* * *

I arrived back home, made cheese on toast, and ate it in bed.

I spent a while replaying some of our museum scenes. I was getting hooked on Cooper and he had the power to mess with my head even when he wasn't around. I was also just really horny. I thought about his shoulders, and the curly hair on his forearms.

I reached over for my bag and pulled out the treasure he'd stolen for me and placed the items tidily on my bedside table. Dinosaur toys from the gift shop.

I'm a fucking scientist, not a child.

But it was also romantic. No-one had stolen anything for me before. I got my phone and started replying to the texts he'd sent me. The conversation started innocently enough but descended quickly into smutty fantasies. We agreed to meet again that weekend, and I went to sleep a hot mess.

after

Outside the airport, I was lost in my memories as I arranged the supplies. "This is great!" Laguna announced as she reappeared around the corner of the airport building.

I squealed and jumped to my feet.

"I didn't mean to startle you, sorry."

"I was just in the zone."

"I can see that." Laguna's voice sounded impressed and that pleased me more than I wanted.

I had organised the materials into tidy piles, separated by size and shape, and then packed everything into smaller boxes and bags that a person could carry. Even the discarded items were neatly stored away in a big container in case they might come in useful for another day. I had found a skill that I could offer, and I liked the feeling of being useful.

The rest of the group appeared behind Laguna and those who still had space, filled their bags and arms with cables and sheets of metal. Once we were carrying everything we could, we began making our way back through the corridors of the airport.

We reached the waiting lounge with the dinosaur exhibit, and I was sorely tempted to take another look. I could have spent a whole day reading the panels, caressing bones, running my fingers over fossilised feathers, and imagining what the world really looked and felt like in their time.

I pushed my shoulders back and adjusted my backpack. *Another time*, I decided. Back to the village to pay off my debts and then back to the beach where I belonged.

"Let's go home?" Laguna asked everyone. I nodded.

And in that moment the building began to tear itself apart.

* * *

Our collective panic was tangible. I had to will myself not to freeze.

The ground beneath the airport shook so hard that several villagers fell to one knee, and I nearly joined them. Dust was falling from the metallic rafters above us and there was a painful groaning as the building adjusted to the moving earth. Dark strip lights swung wildly from the ceiling above us.

This quake was bigger than any I had felt, and we were in exactly the wrong place.

The floor-to-ceiling windows facing out onto the runway groaned then shattered, hurling glass shards all over the benches. We moved as one away from them, towards the centre of the room. Pigeons flew all around us and made their escape through the new opening and we knew we had to do the same.

Laguna made the call.

"Onto the runway!" she shouted, her legs already in motion. "Watch out for the glass!"

The last thing I saw as we climbed out of the window were the bones of *Microraptor, Anchiornis* and *Eosinopteryx* collapsing into the dust.

* * *

We stood on the runway, our bodies shaking as much from fear as from the moving earth. The building ahead of us creaked and groaned and threatened. Dust billowed out of the open space that was once windows, and I wondered if the airport might be finally destroyed in front of our eyes. Then, as suddenly as it had begun, the shaking stopped.

The dust cloud began to clear. I became vaguely aware that, somewhere deep inside the building, an alarm was going off and the sound brought me back. I began to re-inhabit my body. A small flock of crows was passing over us, their calls speaking to the deepest part of my gut. I looked around and remembered that I wasn't alone there.

The villager who I knew only as the storyteller, the one who had taught us about the origins of Sasu, was bleeding from a cut on their leg. Without a word, another villager pulled off their backpack, knelt down, and took out a first aid kit. I watched as they struggled to put on latex gloves, cleaned the wound briefly with alcohol and removed a tiny piece of glass with tweezers. Although the person was competent, I would have done it better. I would have cleaned more, bandaged tighter. The dressing wouldn't survive the journey back to the village and I knew it.

I just stared and watched it happen.

I had patched myself up countless times in the last years. From sheer necessity I had developed my own first aid protocols and techniques. I was a hundred miles away from being a doctor, but I was thousand times better than this person.

I also know now that when I'm scared and stressed, I tend to judge everyone and everything. It's a control thing, it's terrible but it helps.

In that moment, the instinct to take care of others, which was an integral part of the Imperative, just wouldn't translate in my body. I could have helped; instead, I watched. I would have done it better. I didn't. And I was filled with an inexplicable rage.

"Are we all okay?" Laguna asked, turning to look at each of us.

I was shocked by the strength of my own voice. "How *can* we be? We nearly died!"

My voice trembled and I was shouting. And the embarrassment of that realisation just made me angrier.

"Why am I even here, putting my life in danger for you people? I don't owe you a fucking thing!"

Laguna locked my eyes with hers. Her expression of surprise relaxed into something softer. For a moment I felt tied to her in a way that was physical and threaded through with power.

She visibly took a deep breath and my body mirrored hers. She dropped her shoulders and mine fell too.

Another breath and something moved. It was my imagination—it had to be—but my feet tightened inside of my shoes to grasp onto the earth as that mysterious something dropped down and left me behind.

I shook. I breathed.

I was still angry, and my thoughts raged on—*it isn't my village that needs a new fence. How much do I have to give before I'll be forgiven?* But the thoughts had lost some of their strength.

For a moment I remembered the exhibit inside, buried now under dust and rubble. I was glad I got to see it. I looked around me at the others, dusting off their clothes, offering each other hugs and shaking silently. *We experienced this together, I'm not alone.*

Laguna turned towards the horizon. "We need to check on the others."

* * *

The young person who took care of the chickens met us at the edge of the village.

"Are you okay?" Laguna asked them.

They told us that the tremors had barely been felt in the village. The chickens had gotten nervous just before the quake started, but they were okay too. I could see a few pecking around in their enclosure, scratching in the hay like nothing had happened.

"There's dinner," they informed us before turning back to the village.

As we entered the village circle, we saw the plates of freshly cooked food that had been laid out for us.

"The most precious of all direct actions," I heard the storyteller whisper to Laguna.

An early fire was burning, and the smell of eucalyptus filled the late afternoon air. Chairs had been set up for us. But no-one sat. We couldn't yet. To be still with these feelings of stress and panic would be to deny our animal need to discharge; to integrate and reset.

As one, we kicked off our shoes and continued walking, straight out into the marsh. Our calves were wet within seconds, the boggy earth sucking our feet in with slurps and smacks and gurgles. We headed for the dark waters of the stream.

I lined up with the others along the edge of the riverbank: a rare piece of solidity nestled among the wet land. We took one single moment together among the grasses and reeds to prepare. To hold what had been and what was yet to come. To contemplate what it meant to transition from one event to the next and to stay present throughout. To remember what it meant to breathe. I looked down into the shaded water below me, holding its mysteries. I closed my eyes and jumped.

before

My emotions were coming in waves. I groaned loudly enough to disturb the neighbours and I couldn't have cared less. I felt high, not because of anything pharmaceutical, which has never been my thing, but from the sheer lust and intoxicating scent of Cooper above me as he thrust himself against my chest.

We had been at it for hours by this point. I was thirsty, fatigued, my whole body was sore. But I had no intention of stopping while it still felt this good. I wiggled up towards the wall and guided him into me again. Nothing seemed to make him quit, he'd been hard since we started— out on his giant balcony, with wine and spaghetti and my foot on his crotch.

I kissed him like it was the last time I would ever feel his chiselled face and sandpaper stubble under my tongue. Like I would never again sense his heat against my body or his hair in my fingers.

I drank up every second.

after

The cold water was electric to my body. Every part of my skin buzzed; my face was charged until suddenly there was nothing. No thoughts. No worries, memories, or projections of futures unknown. Only intensity and downward movement and when I reached it, the squishy mud between my toes was an embrace.

The water was deep, and my instinct was to push back up immediately to return to the familiar air.

I stayed.

I had a sense of receiving a precious gift that I wasn't ready to let go of yet. Until I had to. Exploding out of the water, my hands held high, the inhale felt like my first and the world was completely alive.

Which of course is the point. As embodied people have always known, intensity is rebirth, and life without ritual is a dark forest with no path and no touchstones to remember the way.

What else is there? I wondered as I soaked up that expansive moment of merging and emerging and feeling every part of my body as if it was brand new.

My body sang to me, and I was enthralled by the harmony. Other than the cold of the water and fresh air pouring into my lungs, my senses were all turned inward. In that moment I knew myself in pristine detail.

And finally, when I was ready to come back and share my consciousness with other beings again, I looked around me and saw the others. They were already back on the grassy shore of the stream, chatting and bathing and drying in the warm sun. How long had I been gone? I was the only one still in the water.

Then embarrassment and shame came. Social habits pressed in on me to worry about what other people thought of me, to judge myself by what others did.

I wanted to worry and remember.
I wanted to leave this tender moment.
But in that same instant, I knew all these things as companions.
Fleeting parts of myself to be taken care of.
I thanked shame and judgement and I let them go.
I smiled at my new friends and dropped back down under the water.

Wet and panting, I collapsed onto the bed next to Cooper. The bed had lost all its sheets, duvet, and pillows. There was just the two of us, sprawled over each other, limbs entwined. He kissed my neck; he licked my arms. My world was full of his smell and touch. Until suddenly it wasn't.

Cooper left the bed so quickly it felt aggressive. He stood up abruptly without even a pretence of transition. I watched him observing me, my exposed body, with such unblinking intensity that for a moment I wished the duvet was within reach.

"Okay?" I asked him.

"Wine?" he asked me.

I didn't have time to answer before he turned and left.

We had spent an entire night in various levels of synchronisation and there was no way for me not to feel that change. No way to stop panic from filling my chest.

"I'm out here," he called me a few minutes later from the balcony.

I slipped into his bathrobe and made my way to him.

* * *

"I don't want this to be a thing," he informed me as he filled my glass. I wasn't in the mood to drink more but I took it anyway.

"Cooper, what's happening?"

"No, it's fine," he said. "I don't want to fight."

Who's fighting?

I racked my brain, trying to understand. "Wasn't the sex good for you?"

"It was fine." He finished his wine and reached for the bottle.

"Really? You came like five times. I thought we were having fun. Why didn't you say someth—?"

Cooper interrupted me with the loud popping of the cork. He poured himself another drink and looked directly at me. Glared might be a more accurate word.

"Look," he said, still holding eye contact. "It was hot and then, I don't know, it wasn't anymore. But don't make a big deal out of it. You were tired or something. Or drunk, but it's fine."

I stared for a moment at the glass of wine in my hand. It was only my second of the night.

"I'm not drunk or tired. I mean I'm a bit sleepy, but we've been having sex since yesterday." My voice was too high; defensive, desperate. "Did I do something wrong? I don't understand, Cooper."

He shrugged. "Maybe you should go home then if you're tired."

I collected my things and left. I spent the entire walk home in a storm of thoughts. Maybe I *was* tired? Maybe the wine had hit me harder than I thought? We hadn't eaten much, but I felt fine. What was going on?

My mind was so busy, I almost took a wrong turning a few blocks from my flat. Something wasn't right here.

I don't really know what I'm doing," I said, a hammer in my hand, staring at the fencepost like it was an artifact from another world. Another night and morning had passed since we returned from the airport, since that orgasmic reset in the stream. I was still in the village. I had thought about leaving quietly when I woke up that morning, but I like to finish things—even if it meant another day away from home. I knew that the thought of an unfinished project would scratch my brain for weeks.

We'd complete the fence, protect the village from night-dogs—or whatever else—and I would go home at last. That was the new plan. And yes, I knew on some level how ridiculous it was to keep trying to leave and making plans to go home.

Laguna touched my shoulder so lightly I wasn't even sure it happened. But the tingle down my spine was real.

"It's perfect," she replied, and her words soothed me. "Just be sure to hammer the nails down over the wire so that it's fixed to the post."

"Like this?" I asked, feeling uncertain and vulnerable at the same time. I knocked a nail into the wood halfway, just a few millimetres below the wire and then hit it a bit softer to bend it over. Bending nails, I had found, was much easier than hitting them straight in.

"One more hit to be sure," Laguna said. The head of the nail dug into the wood, and I could see that the wire was now secure. Which was obvious really and I have no idea why I doubted myself so much with these things. I lived by myself in a cave. I had survived all kinds of traumatic events. Yet a simple hammer and nails could make me feel like a ten-year-old again, expected to be able to do all kinds of things in the world and finding all of them formidable.

Laguna was smiling at me. "I used to hate everything DIY as well," she confided as if she knew my every thought. "We call it DIT here, as in 'do-it-together', which only makes it slightly less awful."

I smiled too. "You seem so natural at these things."

"I learned. We all learned. But, Brook..." She rarely used my name, and I instantly paid more attention. "We don't *all* need to do *all* the things. Even now. If you hate this, there are a hundred other tasks to do in the village, and I'd always rather we be doing the things we love than the things we don't. The world should have enough room for all our passions."

I looked at the fence post again and at the heavy hammer in my hand. I gripped the handle a little tighter.

"Challenges are good sometimes," I told her, but also myself. "Let me see how far I get, and I'll call you if I get stuck?"

Laguna squeezed my shoulder. "I'll come back and check on you in half an hour. Have fun."

She turned and left me to my hammering.

* * *

I wish I had been fully present during the fence construction because it could have been beautiful. I found I was able to coordinate well with the other villagers. When someone would approach me, spooling a line of wire behind them, I stepped out of the way automatically. When it was time to hammer more nails, a path was cleared for me to get to work. I finally figured out the perfect angles needed to knock nails into posts, and we were finished with the fence, and even a make-shift gate, before sunset. It could have been so satisfying.

But it wasn't what I was thinking about.

Laguna said she'd come back in half an hour and the day was already getting old. *She's forgotten about me, again.*

It's fine, I decided. *I don't even need her.* I stood behind the new fence, watching the red sun reflect off the taught wires. I was filled with disappointment. *Why did she do that? Why would she lie to me?*

Then a dropping sensation as if the ground had disappeared.

I'm still here. I was trapped in the village, and I could never go home. *Why can't I leave?*

The dinner bell rang, and I turned to face the village circle without thinking. My mind filled with images of thick slices of fresh bread. I had to get out of here. And I would never trust Laguna's word again.

I was cornered. I didn't know what to do.

Cooper had left me *seventeen* voice messages apologising—which I considered to be at least sixteen too many. I had to understand how sorry he was. He was tired, like me. Probably a bit drunk—like me. Surely, I understood.

One message was an attempt at a joke—about how it was all my fault really for exhausting him with the amazing sex.

I knew that my boundaries, and my head, were being messed with. I knew that I would have to suck up my fear and just tell him it was over. I would miss him, and his strong arms and the smell of coconut shampoo on his perfect hair, but he obviously wasn't the sweet guy he presented himself as.

I also knew men like him well enough to know that this had already gone too far and there was no way he would let it finish well. He would fight it to the end.

I decided to tell him on the phone because text would be too impersonal. Underneath it all he was sensitive, and I didn't want to hurt him, just protect myself from the glimpses of the handsome monster I'd seen after our perfect day together. On the third ring, he picked up.

"Brook!" he practically shouted. I held the phone a bit further from my ear. "So glad you called. Wanna come over?"

His words were slurred. He was drinking.

"I can't right now. I'm out," I lied.

"I really need to talk to you, babe."

"I got your messages." I tried to sound firm. "Cooper, it really wasn't okay what you said on the balcony. I feel like you blamed me for something that I didn't do."

"I know babe!" He shouted again. "And I promise it won't happen again. Look, just come over and we'll talk about it, okay? I'll cook."

For whatever reason, despite my screaming intuition, that evening I found myself again on Cooper's balcony.

after

As I sat down on the grass with the rest of the village, my head was busy. I was hurting and I was ashamed about it. Laguna arrived carrying two plates. She sat down, passed me one and began eating.

"We finished the fence," I said flatly, as I poked my salad with a fork.

"That's great!" she enthused. I knew her face was bright, but I refused to look up from my plate.

"I did it without you."

I felt Laguna shifting. "Okay," she said, obviously confused. "Did you need me for something?"

"No," I huffed, embarrassed my own childish tone. "I was fine."

"Okay..."

We sat in silence for a moment. Laguna ate, and the sounds of food in her mouth disturbed me. I bit into a cherry tomato, fresh from the garden. It was too acidic and hurt my tongue.

"Did something happen?" she tried again. "Is everything okay?"

"You said you'd come back to check on me and you didn't." I looked up at her and steadfastly ignored her expression of confusion. "I mean why did you say that, if you weren't going to do it?"

She breathed. "I got waylaid, sorry. One of the chickens had escaped and we needed to help someone who's having a medical thing right now and... anyway I'm sorry. I guess I didn't realise it was important and figured that if you needed me, you'd come find me."

"I didn't need you."

"Okay."

I held her eye contact now. My heart was speeding up. "I just don't like overpromising. You said we'd be safe in the airport too, and we weren't. Not even close."

Laguna looked thoughtful as if trying to recall her words. "*When* did I say that?"

"At lunch, yesterday. When you announced the mission."

"Did I say, we'd be safe or that we *should* be safe? There hadn't been a tremor in months."

"Same difference."

I could see that she didn't agree.

"I'm sorry," she said then.

Apologies are weird, I remember thinking. How could those words change anything?

I resigned myself to just letting it go—as long as it didn't happen again. I managed to finish my meal, but I fell silent, and Laguna drifted off into conversations with other people. I went to bed angry that night and between disturbed dreams I ran over the conversation a thousand times. My words, her words, the words that weren't said but should have been. Maybe I was wrong about the airport thing, but she was definitely supposed to check on me. Why would people say one thing but do another?

I was determined to never feel that vulnerable again.

before

Maybe I had misjudged Cooper after all. He brought me a delicious meal to the balcony, lit a candle, laid out napkins and everything. I knew he was making an effort. He served me a generous glass of wine, and I noticed he was drinking cola and had sobered up somewhat. There was a band playing in the street and little snatches of beats and song reached us. We ate quietly, but it didn't feel awkward.

That lasted all of ten minutes.

"Brook," he said after we'd finished eating. He put his cutlery down in a weird, over-controlled way. "I need you to forgive me for last night. I'm hurt that you didn't respond to my messages."

I felt my shoulders lifting. "I did respond! I called you. I'm here now, aren't I?"

He sighed and ran his finger along the edge of his plate.

"It took a lot for me to apologise, you know." He paused. "Especially when I didn't really do anything wrong."

I didn't know how to respond. I took a breath and replied, "I still don't understand what happened. I thought we had a good day together?"

He crossed his arms. "It was good. You're hot. But I..." His face shifted. I could see he was battling with something and almost felt bad for him. "I'm scared I guess."

"Of me?"

"Of you changing."

I was perplexed. "Changing?"

He leaned forward. It wasn't overtly hostile, but I felt myself withdrawing into my chair.

"You said you're trans, right?"

I nodded. My chest tightened.

"And, well the thing is, Brook. I like your body just how it is. I don't want you to change it."

A thousand thoughts ran through my mind in that moment.

I shouldn't have told him. It's not his choice.

And, more importantly, if he felt he was entitled to express opinions—even make decisions—over my body, what else was he capable of? The alarms going off in my mind for days were finally making it through the fog of lust.

"I think I'm going to go home," I managed to squeeze out, although my throat was tight. "I have work in the morning."

Cooper stood up then, so abruptly that his chair fell back and hit the balcony floor with a crash.

"That's fine." Then his voice softened. "Just remember, you promised me."

I felt myself retreating further but tried to stay calm. "What did I promise you Cooper?"

"Yesterday. You said we were going to do some kinky stuff together. You said there were things you wanted to explore with me. With the whip and my suit and all that."

I remembered the conversation, but it was hardly a promise. And something as intimate and dangerous as sex never can be. I stood softly and backed slowly into the living room.

"Oh that, of course!" I said, but even to me it sounded fake. "We'll definitely do that. Next time. That sounds really hot." I continued backing away and picked up my jacket without looking away from him.

"Tomorrow?" he asked, his voice vulnerable again.

"Definitely." I slipped on my shoes.

"Your place?"

"Definitely."

"You'll text me your address?"

I tried not to say definitely. "I'll text you my address." Then, with the sexiest smile I could muster I said, "Make sure you dress up for me."

Cooper smiled as he approached me next to the door. "Oh, I will."

He kissed me on the cheek, and I felt myself freeze.

"See you tomorrow, babe."

As I turned the corner into the stairwell, I felt him watching me. Then I ran down the stairs and out of the building and I didn't stop running until I was back home.

after

The sky was still dark as I went to the village circle and found Laguna doing something to the water pump with a rusty wrench. "I'm leaving today," I announced to her. My voice was steel, and it had to be.

Laguna looked up and her eyes were wide. "Morning Brook."

I didn't know if she hadn't heard me, or she was trying to make a point about my directness. I tried again.

"I'm going to tidy up the tent and head back to my cave. It's time for me to leave."

Laguna put down the wrench, stood and faced me. "Do you need help?"

"I don't really have anything to pack," I said, softening. "But I'd like to strip the bed and tidy up the tent. And if I can take some supplies, that would be helpful."

I didn't need her for any of those things, but it would be easier to have her there. The village had a mysterious power over me and breaking the inertia was already difficult enough.

Laguna nodded. "Sure thing. After breakfast?"

"Yes please."

"No problem."

Breakfast came and went. I returned to my tent—which would soon no longer be 'my' tent—and had everything tidied and orderly within ten minutes. I went to the supply tent and filled my backpack with enough food to get me through the next weeks. I took an office water bottle and filled it at the tap.

And still there was no sign of her.

I knew I was being impatient. But she'd also said, 'after breakfast' and it was very much after breakfast. The sun was getting high in the sky. My body felt tight, and my shoulders ached as I hefted the heavy backpack onto them. I turned towards the gate we'd installed in the fence and decided to leave there and then without saying goodbye.

I had just reached the gate when I felt Laguna running behind me.

"Brook!" she shouted, breathless. "Are you leaving?"

For a moment I thought of just walking through the gate without a word. Instead, I turned, holding the water bottle between us as a barrier.

"Sorry," she said. She arrived and stood close to me. A bit too close really. "I got caught up. There was a small fire in the kitchen and the chickens got out again and..."

I pursed my lips and crossed my arms tighter.

"You said you'd help me, and you didn't."

Laguna's hand reached for her wrist before she caught herself and forced herself to stay open.

"Sorry."

I lost control.

"What does that even *mean* though? Sorry doesn't help me! I can't eat your apologies. You say one thing, but you do another. How can I trust that? How can I trust *you*?"

Laguna breathed in that way she did a lot in those days. Deep, controlled and shamelessly taking all the time she needed.

"Brook. I didn't know you were leaving straight away. I have a lot of responsibilities here and I got pulled into other things. And honestly—" She paused, and this time grabbed her wrist firmly. "—I don't really want you to go."

Something moved between us. My anger was draining out of me, replaced by another sensation—a painful and vulnerable feeling in my chest.

"But I need to leave."

"I know. I just...you fit so well here. People really appreciate you. I appreciate you. I guess, I hoped you might make your home here with us."

It was a lot to take in. That vulnerable feeling was expanding, and I was deeply uncomfortable.

"I'll visit in a few weeks to get supplies," I offered. "If that's okay."

Laguna smiled. "Of course."

There was a pause.

"And Brook?"

"Yes?"

"Feel free to come in the front entrance this time."

I turned and left. Laguna closed the gate behind me.

before

By the time I arrived back at my apartment, in a whirlwind of panic, sweat and exhaustion, Cooper had already left me three more voice messages. I deleted them without listening. Feeling defiant, I switched off my phone and put it in a kitchen cupboard in case anxiety got the better of me during the night.

I stood for a while watching the world go by down below. It had started raining and I opened the window to let in some fresh air and hopefully blow away some of my feelings. It didn't help.

I knew that he wouldn't stop messaging. I knew that now, more than ever, Cooper expected more from me than I could give him. He would push for us to meet again as soon as possible. *I should have told him how I really felt. There were so many warnings.*

But as I watched the rain get heavier and the streetlights blur, I also knew that whatever happened, I wasn't to blame. Or at least not entirely. While I had been too enthralled to notice my own alarm bells, Cooper was the one who treated me like a piece of meat. While I could have been more direct, we do what we need to, to survive.

Sleep didn't come easy that night. I half expected him to knock on my door, which was absurd, now I come to think of it. It was a big city and, for whatever reason—instinct or just an abundance of caution—I had never given him my address. I don't think I even told him which neighbourhood I lived in.

The next morning, I woke up exhausted, feeling heavy and flat. It was still raining, and I found it hard to get my day started. *I should get ready for work. I should change my phone number.*

I'm sure that Cooper would have found ways to chase me for a very long time. I'm sure the drama would have drawn on, breaking my heart, and sending my anxiety through the roof.

But in the end, none of it mattered. The world, as we knew it, ended that afternoon.

149

after

With determination and an angry rhythm in my hips, I marched out into the bog.

I stomped my feelings out through each angry step. I knew I felt guilty for the number of times I had tried, but failed, to leave. I questioned my own integrity—what good were my intentions, plans and statements if I didn't follow them through? What did it say about me if I decided whole-heartedly on one thing, but ended up doing another?

And what did Laguna mean that she *appreciated* me? What was I supposed to do with that information?

On some level I also had the sense that these questions weren't relevant. I couldn't go back now, and I knew it. I stormed across the soggy marshland, and I began to wonder why I had chosen this path home.

Over years of raiding the village I had my route mapped out clearly in my mind: cross the meadow, over or around the hill, through the patchy forest and bracken, down the cliff to the beach, turn west and head towards home.

Only once had I tried walking between home and the village via the marsh. The experiment had ended abruptly as the mud reached up to my chest. My arms had been scratched to pieces as I had pulled myself out of a deep spot and had fallen straight onto a bank of brambles. I spent a week sneezing and vowed never to take that route again.

And yet, here I was, navigating the few dry spots between ponds and moss-covered mud, my feet already soaked, and my arms burning with mosquito bites. I couldn't tell you why I chose the difficult path that day. Maybe it offered a more direct route back to my home and the safety of solitude, or maybe I just wanted to punish myself.

The mud practically destroyed my only pair of trainers. By the time I reached the area where the bog opened up into a shallow estuary and the cool brackish water lapped around my calves, I began to weep. Partly because of pain and exhaustion and partly because the sight of the sea spreading out ahead of me reminded me of everything I had sacrificed for that week in the community. As I continued walking, mud gradually faded into sand, and I was soon back on my beach.

Despite my aching muscles and the heavy backpack and water bottle, I started running. Now that I was so close, I couldn't be away from home for another minute. I grinned and laughed as the sea breeze messed my hair and blasted sand against my face. I could see the five white stones that marked the entrance to my cave. I was nearly home! Security beckoned—now just a few minutes away.

As I arrived and dropped everything I was carrying onto the sand, I bent over to catch my breath. I became aware of blood running down my left thigh, a cut I hadn't noticed. And slowly, as though still walking through heavy mud, I took in the devastation that was once my home.

3. flight

during

It's difficult for me to tell the story of what happened after Cooper. It was a dark period for all of us and some of the things I was driven to do for survival might shock you. Unless you've been through that too.

I guess it was an unhealthy diet of disaster movies when I was a kid that convinced me that I'd be the good one in the story: the protagonist who shows up to the challenge and comes out stronger. The one who defends the community and saves the day. It didn't turn out like that.

The crisis had been rolling on for a while and at some point, many of us had accepted that it was all going to hell. And yet we had also tried to continue life as usual: going to work, going on dates, trying to numb the unacceptable knowledge of what was coming. People have described denial as a narcotic. If so, we were all so addicted that we could no longer imagine life without its desensitising bliss.

Somewhere along the line, I had given up hoarding food and medicine. It's not that I thought we'd seen the worst of it. If anything, our time in lockdown made it clearer to me that I was on the right track. But when I stopped living with Adam, I no longer brought home extra bags of coffee or stored bottles of water behind the sofa. Without a little brother figure to take care of, I just didn't have it in me anymore.

And there was another element that I couldn't quite put my finger on. It felt strange to be prepping just for myself. Where was community in my plans? Surely individuals piling up cans of beans for themselves or their families couldn't be a real solution to anything. I lost inspiration, I gave up, and I'm not sure it would have made much difference.

By day four, groups of armed men started smashing storefronts in the street below me.

By day five, the bottom two floors of my building had been set on fire.

By day seven, I was living out of a backpack, sleeping in parks, and fighting for my life.

* * *

I discovered that when faced with relentless fear, it's possible for tension and vigilance to become routine. Life without them becomes a dark memory, slippery to grasp. After some days, I began to tune out the gunshots and explosions all around. Soon, the dropping panic that awoke me sweating in the night became a timeless part of my existence.

I hid the best I could: difficult in open city spaces barely vegetated with lilac bushes and eucalyptus trees. I moved from park to park, sleepless in a different place each night.

I could have moved less. I could have scouted the area, found safer places to get food, made alliances with other people moving through the parks. I could have assessed my resources and made better plans.

But everything felt like it was in movement back then. Chaos, certainly, but also fluidity. I was living in the moment, making decisions second to second. I couldn't plan past my next meal.

In another time for another person, immersion in the moment and returning to animal instincts could have been an attractive goal. I feel like people have paid good money to be dropped into the wilderness with only a penknife and a compass. Shipwrecked passengers surviving together on an island. Celebrities battling it out in a forest.

It was a fever dream I couldn't wake from. A nightmare of spiralling dread not helped by the fact that all around me, in every park and every street corner, there were birds, dead and dying, scattered among the rosebushes and post-boxes. The new flu was laying waste to wild bird populations as societal collapse was tearing through ours. Most humans had some immunity to H5N1 since the last wave, but for the birds it was a massacre.

* * *

Of all the pandemics of the last decades, bird flu is the one I remember most vividly, perhaps because these very tangible experiences of death all around me in the parks were so different to the relative luxury of staying at home, or the blur of memory that was losing my parents so young. Or perhaps because birds had accompanied me my whole life, even when my own species had felt like a constant source of threat and their loss felt more personal.

The virus had been with us for a while. In the early 2000s, avian flu crossed over to humans several times and looked set to become the next pandemic. Sixty percent mortality, hundreds dead: it had our full attention. Then for a time, it was no longer discussed in terms of human lives, but those of domestic chickens, ducks, and geese. Industrialised chickens couldn't be allowed outside for fear of contamination and free-range eggs disappeared from the supermarket shelves. Mass culling became commonplace. Billions were killed by the virus, or otherwise gassed or asphyxiated by foam.

And a parallel, silent apocalypse had ripped through wild bird populations, ignored by all but a few birdwatchers and conservationists. During the 20s, it crossed over into mammals. Six hundred sealions were found dead in Peru. Mink farms in Spain were ravaged and shut down. Seabirds piled up on the world's beaches and entire species went extinct. Only when it crossed back to humans again did the majority of people start to pay attention.

Then, in the mysterious ways of viruses, H5N1 disappeared from the news cycles and perhaps from the planet. As far as we could tell, poultry—and people—had developed some form of resistance and the virus had stopped mutating. We gladly forgot and moved on, although for the great skua, the Bewick's swan, and the puffin it was already too late. Too few mourned their loss.

* * *

For myself, survival in the parks was all about staying clean enough. Maintaining hygiene was more important to me than eating—hand gel and clean water were my highest priorities. With my immune system as weak as it is, I was never supposed to survive the apocalypse.

The only advantage to any of this was the sharper understanding I gained of what people around me had always experienced.

I had been poor, but always had a warm bed. I had worked from a young age but gotten by with legal work. Homelessness was always 'just a few paycheques away', but I was learning that that was far enough for it to have stayed abstract, not quite a real threat. I was beginning to understand how vicious the system I'd grown up in—and been a part of—could really be.

During those weeks of hell, I have never been more aware of the world, its flavours and complexities. There were furtive interactions, trading one stolen item for another. And there were encounters that were intensely more violent. I have never felt more threatened or alone.

* * *

I slept one night under a particularly thick hawthorn on a hillside. The gnarly old tree had given me some protection against the wind and kept me out of sight, at least until morning. The wooded hill led down to an overgrown lawn where I had picnicked once with Adam. An artificial stream flowed down through the trees, cascading over boulders, and ending in a fiberglass pond. I'd heard the stream running all night, and the sound had been relaxing in its way, although I'm not sure if it was the sound of the water or the memories of Adam that had comforted me.

I startled awake as I heard footsteps on dry leaves. Two strangers were approaching me from the park below.

"Hey friend," said one of them. "Good morning."

I stared at them, only half-awake. I clutched the edge of my sleeping bag, as if that would somehow keep me safe. I made a quick survey of the ground around me: the pepper spray I kept to hand was nowhere to be found.

"Hey," I said, in a voice that I hoped was relaxed but firm. "Are we okay?"

I know it's an odd question, but everything about human interaction at that time felt strange. I had heard a few people asking this question and it seemed like it was becoming a phrase in itself: a way of assessing danger, deescalating tension. We needed anything we could get.

Both of the strangers nodded. "We're okay," the person told me and offered a non-threatening smile.

The other person dropped their backpack gently to the ground. They looked towards me, without making eye contact and asked softly: "Are you hungry?"

I wasn't close to trusting these people. In general, there just wasn't a lot of trust around. But I hadn't eaten for a day or two and I felt like I didn't have a lot of choice. These two strangers were already here, and my pepper spray was lost. By the time I could wiggle out of my sleeping bag, if they wanted to hurt me, it would already be done.

"I could eat," I said, forcing a cautious smile. "I'm Brook."

"Sam, and this is Heather."

Sam had a gentle face and gentle eyes. Heather was a head taller than Sam, and maybe a few years older. Of the two of them, I sensed that Heather had seen much more of the world. She seemed tired and more cautious. Sam reminded me of a younger version of myself from a more innocent time.

Heather opened her backpack and took out, of all things, a frying pan, and a bag of vegetables. She saw my surprise and said, dryly, "Breakfast is served. I'll make us a fire." She stood up and started moving around the park, collecting twigs and branches.

Sam sat down, cross legged, a cautious distance away. They seemed to sense that I was nervous and, as if dealing with a frightened animal, spoke softly. Or maybe they always talked like that, I had no way to know.

"How has it been for you?" Sam asked me.

"It's okay," I said, my tone unconvincing. "I mean, I'm getting by."

"Glad to hear it." Sam reached a hand into their backpack, then paused and looked up at me. "I'm just getting some water out of my bag. Would you like some?"

I appreciated the warning and offer.

"Yes, please."

They passed me a bottle of supermarket brand fizzy water and I drank so fast that bubbles went up my nose.

"Thanks." I wiped my mouth with the back of my hand. I immediately started to feel better and decided to lean in to this strange interaction. "Are you two from around here?"

"We lived in the north of the city, but we've been moving around a lot."

I nodded. "Same."

"Actually, we just moved into a new place with some others last week. It might be good for you too. It's kind of a collective squat situation."

I made a non-committal sound. I was far from comfortable sleeping alone in parks, but nothing about a collective squat situation sounded tempting either.

Heather returned with a handful of sticks and soon had a good fire going. She made a makeshift stand for the frying pan out of thicker branches, poured some oil from a jam jar, and started frying up the veg. Sam dug around in their backpack again, this time for plates.

While they were busy, I decided it was a good moment to get out of my sleeping bag. As relaxed and careful as these strangers seemed to be, I didn't take my eyes off them as I stood slowly, stuffed my bag into my pack and sat back down. I dug around discretely in the leaf litter behind me with one hand and found the pepper spray. I stashed it in my jacket pocket, just in case.

The food was ready, and Heather passed me a plate and a fork. I couldn't imagine why they were both moving around the city with an extra plate in their bag, but I ate gratefully and offered them a smile.

"So," said Heather, as she chewed on her food. "How are you liking the apocalypse so far?"

* * *

Sam gave Heather a look and asked me, "Or maybe a better question—have you noticed that you've been feeling different?"

I didn't know how to answer. In the last few weeks—or maybe months—life had been turned upside down. Of course, I felt different. We all did.

Sam saw my hesitation and added. "Have you noticed your senses changing?"

I took a moment to think.

My senses. In a way, that was impossible to know too. I didn't normally live in public spaces or need to defend myself in the middle of the night from armed strangers. My senses were certainly more honed, but for sheer survival.

And yet, somehow, I understood what they meant. I looked up at the hawthorn spreading out above and around us. I knew my choice to sleep under them wasn't random. They were beautiful, and old, their branches sheltered countless tangled lichens and moist mosses. I had felt safe under them for a reason.

A blackbird flew through the park releasing her rattling call and I knew, beyond knowing, that she had detected a predator, a fox maybe, and was warning the rest of her bird family.

Even the artificial waterfall had spoken to me in some way that night; the words muffled by plastic.

"Yes," I said then. "I've changed."

"Us too," Sam replied. "And if you're ready, we'd love to show you our new world.".

after

At first, it seemed that there was nothing left except the rain-carved limestone and the wind-swept beach. Everything that I had once so foolishly thought of as *my* space, *my* property, *my* home, was gone.

Once my eyes focused and my head began to clear, I saw the pieces of my previous existence scattered across the beach. My saucepan, half-buried in the sand. My cup and plate and a plastic bottle floating in and out on the gentle surf.

I got closer to the cave entrance and saw that the shelves inside had been destroyed, the wood already reclaimed once from the sea, had been finally reduced to soaked splinters, some strewn across the beach, some carried away for good.

The area in front of the cave, marked by the five sentinel boulders—who had failed in their task—was a mess of tangled ropes and my sleeping bag, torn and soaked. The storm had taken everything. It was over.

If I was another person I would have cried, or shouted, with the overwhelming despair that filled my chest. Or I might have pushed down the feelings, cleared my mind and got busy repairing and rebuilding my life. Instead, I fell to my knees and stared into the abyss of lost safety. I knelt, and I stared, and I stayed.

Time passed and I didn't care to notice it. Night came and went and the cold entering my body was just a sense of pressure at the edge of consciousness, something trying to break in, but failing to reach me. I honestly have no idea how long I was there. I have a vague memory of mosquitoes biting me, of the blood on my thigh drying, but I know I didn't eat or drink anything. The laden backpack I had carried from the village sat in the sand, unopened but attracting crabs.

I don't know where I went. I only remember coming back. The first thing I heard was the sound of my own breathing—shallow, fast and slightly wheezy. Next was smell. The sulphur of rotting seaweed and my own stench of adrenaline. The taste of salt on my tongue. And finally, the dull pain in my fingers that always signalled it was over. I was back.

I'd been through this disembodiment before. Even regularly at certain, particularly intense, times of my life. But still, each time was as disorientating as the first.

Slowly and cautiously, as if at any second the world would narrow again into a tunnel of unconsciousness, I stood and shook myself off. I don't mean this as a metaphor—my body shook from the core.

A disconnected part of my mind knew that was a normal response: just a release of bodily tension. Mice do it after they freeze in fear of a passing predator. Humans sometimes repress it, pushing all that energy inside and messing us up in other ways.

I had given up on supressing my instincts a long time ago and I let my body do what was needed. I don't know how long I stayed there, vibrating, sometimes thrashing, but finally the shakes ebbed, and I was done. I got to my feet.

Then, and only then, standing on the beach, surrounded by catastrophe and a life destroyed, I realised I wasn't alone.

* * *

It was a strange sensation, but somehow, a familiar one. A tingling in my neck that crawled down my spine at a languid pace. A feeling of recognition from one body to another. An image of Laguna flashed through my mind.

But as I turned, she was nowhere to be seen; not on the beach and not standing in the gentle waves that rolled in over the sand. I looked up to the cliff but saw no silhouette to give away her presence. *Why would she even be here?*

I stepped closer to what was once my home. Even from outside, I could see that it was empty. *Then, where? How?*

The tingling came again and this time my eyes were drawn upwards to the red and orange morning sky, sparsely populated with a few drawn out clouds. Venus still sparkled on the horizon, and higher still, a single sky-circler, directly above me, soaring so high I almost couldn't see them.

They spiralled upwards, probably on a warm thermal of air. Typical sky-circler behaviour, I thought to myself. But then a change. I sensed the bird's shadow nearby on the beach but couldn't take my eyes off their descending body as the silhouette grew larger against the sky. For a moment I almost felt fear, as though I were a small mammal and should run for cover. But I couldn't.

They swooped down within barely a few metres of my head before abruptly changing direction. My mind was filled with after-images of splayed-out feathers, lethal talons. The bird banked right and flew past the entrance to my cave. A pass, a quick turn, and then they passed by again. I've spent my life around birds, and it was all such bizarre behaviour, I couldn't really process what was happening, I just watched.

Stranger still, were the continued flushes of sensation moving down my spine. I had a sense of being watched closely. I looked around again to see if a human-person was around, but just then the sky-circler turned sharply and disappeared into my cave.

I waited, confused. Unsure what to do next.

A minute or two passed and Laguna stepped out of the darkness, naked, her face etched with concern.

* * *

Laguna moved towards me, and I couldn't speak.

It wasn't the first time I'd been frozen in her presence, and it wouldn't be the last.

She grew closer; every step across the sand, deliberate and precise.

Regret for the angry words of our last encounter came back to me in a rush. I was relieved to see her, and I was also stunned. The way she walked was different; there was something about her hips, her shoulders. Her gait was all wrong. And, my god, her knees...

Already the effect was fading and by the time she reached me, Laguna looked perfectly like herself again. I realised I wasn't sure if I should look away. We had never seen each other naked before. But I saw nothing of shame or embarrassment in her features. Just deep, deep concern.

"Your home, my love," she said. "I'm so sorry."

No words came to my mind, or my mouth.

"You're probably wondering how I got here."

"The sky-circler..." I said finally. My tongue was thick with dehydration, and shock.

"Yes."

I uncrossed my arms but couldn't remember crossing them. I had a sense that the world couldn't be trusted, as if I was watching my life unfold from outside. None of this could be true. I was dreaming or dead or hallucinating from exposure.

She stepped softly over to the backpack still laying in the sand. Several crabs scuttled away as she sat down and pulled out a lunchbox. Laguna unwrapped a sandwich and held it out to me.

"Sit my love. Drink. I'll explain everything."

* * *

"I had this teacher once, her name was Aleena," Laguna began. I realised I'd been biting my nails and brought my hand down.

"I wasn't formally Aleena's student, but she was my elder in meaningful ways and we both understood that I had a lot to learn from her. Spiritually I mean, and politically."

I nodded. Although my head was buzzing, I felt my body settling in for a new story. I breathed my impatience away and listened as I chewed on the bread.

"Aleena and I had attended an activist gathering together. This was years before the Shift when coal plants were still a thing that needed to be protested and shut down. There was a whole week of direct actions and community engagement and all the good grassroots organising that I thought I was put on this earth for."

"And yet, I was really unhappy. Not just exhausted—because five hundred people in planning meetings and actions is always too much. And not just devastated from the usual state violence. It was something else. I felt isolated. The more people I was around and the less space and time I had to myself, the lonelier I felt. Aleena was there with me, and we even ran a few meetings and workshops together and in so many ways the whole week was this huge success. I mean really, we achieved so much. But I was hurting, and I couldn't understand why."

"It sounds overwhelming," I offered. I couldn't imagine being around that many people for a day, much less a week. My mind wondered back for a moment to the Bunker Blockades and the memory was something physical that threatened to close up my throat. "Too much... responsibility?"

Laguna sighed lightly. "Yeah, that's part of it, you're right. But this was something I'd been struggling with for a while before all of that. Like, sometimes I couldn't be with people, but I also couldn't be without them—do you know that feeling?"

I shrugged but didn't mean to. "I like being alone."

"Really?"

"I mean, away from human-people. I was happy here with the beach and the crabs and my cave."

Laguna smiled. "Which is not the same thing as being alone."

I looked at her for a moment trying to understand.

"Brook, when we're with the *other-people*—" she whispered the words to avoid offending anyone listening "—we're with family. It isn't the same as being alone, not at all."

"But that's what that word means, isn't it? Alone is when we're not with humans."

"Not for us."

"Us...?" I asked. "Shifted?"

"Maybe. But I think it's more than that. You said you lived in a city, right?"

"Yes."

"Did you feel lonely there?"

"All the time," I admitted.

"But also overwhelmed with people?"

I nodded.

"Me too." Laguna's face was full of emotion and her cheeks were flushed. "Every single day. Party-sorrow, we call it now. But when I was away from human-people, on a walk somewhere, just listening to the trees and birds, I didn't feel that way. I felt connected and at home. This was always true, the Shift just amplified it somehow."

"Does Sasu have a word for that too?" I asked curiously.

"I'm not sure we have yet," she replied. "A person can be alone in the sense of having no human-people around but in fact be well accompanied, by others. The bugs and trees and air and birds are always with us, whether we notice them or not, and with so many opportunities to connect, loneliness might not be as inevitable as it sometimes seems. Our species doesn't have a monopoly on companionship. Hawthorn trees and crabs can be reliable friends too."

I watched her quietly, trying to absorb these new ideas. "And your teacher, Aleena?" I asked.

"She taught me that this was okay and nothing to fear. People like her, and me, and I strongly suspect, you, Brook, aren't supposed to be at the centre of human life. And we can't be at the centre of non-human life either. We're a bridge, between two worlds."

I was beginning to understand. It was so simple in a way, Aleena's words through Laguna spoke to me and touched something inside, something deeply familiar and lodged in a hundred memories. In a pre-Shift world, none of it had been possible. Things that made me different, were also things that brought risk and violence.

I was flooded with images of forced friendships and relationships, of trying to fit in to something that made no sense and wasn't built for me. I had been rejected so many times when people caught a glimpse of my real, complex self and I had learned to lock it all up.

Then came memories of calm, sitting petting a friend's cat or losing myself in the details of a sycamore seed, at the back of the school playing field. Out of sight. At the edge. My heart suddenly jumped, and I began to see everything that I had given up because of fear. How much I had shut down, just to survive.

"A bridge," I said, but I could already feel myself losing track of the conversation. My attention was being pulled to the sky and I was distantly aware that my cheeks were wet.

Laguna took my hands and brought me back to her.

"That's why it never worked. Why we never fit in and why so few could embrace us as whole people. We had to sacrifice so much, but our other-people family were here waiting for us all along. We literally call them family now because Sasu and the Shift have changed us. But it was always true, and we felt it more deeply than most. Some human-people never forgot, but most in our culture did."

I felt heavy then. A sense of my body being pulled towards the earth. The sound of Laguna's breathing and the warmth of her hands merging with the countless other sensations reaching my body in that moment. Wind and salt and bird-speak and bee-speak, pollen and sand and stone.

"And, of course," Laguna said softly. "Bridges have two ends."

"And we have...two..." I began but couldn't finish.

Laguna squeezed my hands tighter.

"Yes, my love. You have *two* families. You've never been alone."

* * *

For a while, Laguna and I fell into a comfortable silence. We weren't yet ready for more words or conversation. Other voices reached our ears.

I heard the honking of a small group of geese passing by on their migration route south. I looked up and they were beautiful, forming a perfect V. For a moment, I longed to follow them. The knowledge of approaching winter seeped into my bones, and I shivered in spite of the warm sunshine on my face.

My body ached to go with them on their voyage through the sky and for the tiniest glimpse of a moment, I knew that I could. *I saw Laguna transform. And she said that I...*

I pushed it away. Her words, and Aleena's, described my life accurately. And the metaphor, if that's what it was, of us being bridges between two worlds, felt resonant to my deepest gut. But that certainly didn't mean that we could, that I could... nothing in my science-conditioned brain could accept it. And yet, I believed in evidence, and I'd seen her walking out of my cave. And truth be told, I always knew she was special.

"Brook?" Laguna's soft voice whispered between my thoughts. I looked at her and was transfixed by her mouth. "Do you want me to show you?"

Each word was crisp and enticing and I was lost in the tiniest shine of moisture and muscles and the air between her lips as they formed the words.

I nodded without deciding to. She took my hands and stood up, pulling me to my feet.

And there among the grains of sand and the gusts of wind, with the safety that only a trans person can give another, she taught me how to accept my true self.

* * *

Here is where I will lose words to accurately describe what happened next. It's relatively easy to tell you about jumping into deep, cold water or touching the ancient bone of a dinosaur. You probably know something about being a human watching crabs or eating freshly baked bread. You might have images and memories to put next to some of the stories I've told you. But flying, with my own body, soaring under my own power through moving air? I couldn't have imagined it, although I'd tried many times, and I don't know if I can explain it in a way your body will understand.

But let me try.

First, my sense of self was utterly changed and so at least for me in that moment, everything was different.

Mammals and birds diverged such a long time ago, our bodies barely recognise each other anymore. I flew, and I was no longer ape. Air rushed through my feathers, and I was no longer mammal.

My eyes could perceive ultra-violet for the first time. The land was criss-crossed with glowing lines I had never known. I felt like I could see forever.

My bones, my joints, my hearing—with all that change came instinct. Baby birds from flying species know how to fly as soon as they're ready to try. They might take some convincing, a caring parent to nudge them on their way, but they know. And I knew. My breastbone felt strong, and I felt insulated against the breeze. Every gust of wind spoke to me, and it was beginning to make sense.

Which doesn't mean it was easy. I watched Laguna soaring upwards, adjusting her long flight feathers and couldn't get the same movement in my own wings. I was stuck, suspended, my wings beating the air keeping me perfectly in place.

But of course, that's what wind-hovers do well, and my body's instinct was showing me how to falcon.

Are you okay?

Laguna's words arrived in my mind. From above me she had released a short contact call from her mouth, but in my mammal brain it became words. Or my falcon brain. *What am I? What am I? Fuck.*

I froze. Overwhelm had hit and I pulled my wings towards me. I wanted to cross my arms, hug myself, be protected from so much change. But I didn't have arms and I began to fall.

Brook!

The voice in my mind was sharper now.

Spread your wings. Open up.

I did and I caught myself. Then, without even the ability to choose, I followed Laguna as she descended slowly to the ground. We landed, and I felt my talons connect with sand and pebbles. I breathed out and closed my eyes and we stood there together; two naked mammals alone on the beach.

* * *

I woke up shivering. My body was freezing.

Sometime in the night I had crawled into my cave, pulled together the ferns and what was left of my sleeping bag, and fallen asleep. Bleary-eyed, I looked around at the piles of broken shelves and plastic bags that used to be my home. It was barely light outside, and rain was falling. The sound of the waves felt familiar, and proximity to the sea soothed my tired body, but I was so cold.

I stretched and rolled over. Apparently, I'd had the forethought to bring my bag and supplies in before sleeping. Maybe I knew rain was coming. I couldn't remember getting to bed. I only remembered returning to the beach and seeing the aftermath of the storm. *It wasn't raining then, was it?*

But I ate sandwiches with Laguna. Wait.

Did that happen?

And then all at once, the dream came back to me. *I flew! And Laguna was a bird.*

I was smiling as I stood up to leave my cave. Well, it's not the

171

weirdest dream I've ever had.

I stood for a moment at the entrance watching the rain falling and the waves moving in on to the beach. It was then, as my eyes were drawn down to the white sentinel rocks, that I saw the one closest to me had an object sitting on it. I bent down and picked it up. It was a feathered wing.

I separated a feather and as I've done with feathers my whole life, I rubbed my finger along the edge of the barbs unzipping and zipping them back up. I felt the hollow shaft between my fingers and moved the feather in the light to see its colours. Iridescence. Blues fading into greens into purples. A cream tip. *Sturnus vulgaris*, no doubt about it.

Because after our first flight, Laguna had taught me to hunt.

* * *

I began to fly regularly with Laguna. Each morning she would visit me just after sunrise. I waited for her at the water's edge, taking flight to join her as soon as I felt that familiar tingling, her feathered shadow appearing over the top of the cliff.

I orientated my days around those hours spent together. Each time, we explored something new. Flying higher to try out our incredibly amplified vision. Hunting voles, occasional young birds and, once, a juicy rabbit that we shared on the ground, our feathers bloody and warm.

Today, Laguna was helping me improve my balance in the wind. With her guidance, my confidence was growing, but maintaining control in strong winds was still proving difficult. And self-control, at least as a human, was something I always wanted more of.

We were flying above the cliff edge, maybe forty metres into the air—although my perception of space was no longer quantifiable in that way. The trees were smaller, the clouds closer, and I could see details beyond the treeline. Here the gusts of sea wind smashed into the stiller air held by the edge of the forest. Laguna had chosen the spot specifically because I found it so difficult to maintain equilibrium here. The clashing tides and whirlpools of air confused me, and I had already needed to return to the ground three times since we began.

"Relax," Laguna's voice told me as I struggled through a tight vortex of air that had grabbed my tail and pulled me around. "You're trying too hard."

Once I was stabilised again, I asked, "Relax? How can I relax when I feel like I'm going to fall out of the sky at any moment?"

To be clear, we were communicating vocally. I didn't quite understand how, but a sharp 'Keee' from my beak was enough to transmit all this information to Laguna, soaring above. Maybe all birds can do this—even between species—or maybe it was only us. I have no idea and no way to know. The few other birds I had met in this form had stayed clear of us—or fallen prey to Laguna's deadly talons. And Laguna had told me that other sky-circlers and wind-hovers wouldn't recognise us as members of their species. They knew, and we knew, that we were fundamentally different. Probably. But the mice and voles certainly feared us as much as they would any other predator.

I adjusted my position again and fanned out my tail. I felt like I was gaining stability, and if I tightened the muscles in my chest and my wings and pulled my neck in just so, I would almost have it. Another gust smashed into me, and my left wing was pulled out at a wild angle. I fell until I managed to right myself. I could feel Laguna's concern as she dropped down near me.

"You're too tight," she told me. "I know it's difficult but you're trying to resist. You can't control change; you just need to ride it out."

"Easy to say," I replied. "But how do I do that?"

"Relax. The air is never the same twice. It will always, always change, and we have to change with it. Breathe. Let your body adapt to the moment."

I tried to incorporate Laguna's advice, but with each eddy and stream buffeting my body, I just tightened up more. I was exhausted.

"Keep trying," Laguna told me. "You're still thinking of yourself and the air as two separate entities. But right now, you are part of the sky."

I hovered close to her—the only form of flight that felt instinctual to me—and we made eye contact. I was already becoming accustomed to her bird form, but in the morning light, her eyes were especially beautiful. Her feathers were smooth despite the buffeting wind; her wings beat with power. "Can we take a break?"

"Just a bit longer, you've nearly got it."

And then somehow, as if given permission, I entered trust and flow. For that single moment it was as though we were hovering together through time as well as space. The future and past felt as tangible as earth and sea. I was fully present.

Then a howling gust came out of nowhere, smashed into me, and I fell.

I tumbled towards the trees beneath us and nearly collided with the outstretched branch of a hawthorn, twisting myself out of the way at the last minute. I felt the pain of a tail feather caught on a thorn. I continued to fall, and it was enough to sap the last of my energy.

We set down next to a small stream, and I collapsed into a thicket of ferns. I don't remember changing form, but I must have lost time because my next memory was of my head on Laguna's warm, naked lap, her fingers combing through my hair. I didn't even try to get up and let exhaustion take control, pulling me down into confused dreams of impossible wind and wild, red berries.

during

Birds were everywhere. Sunlight cascaded down through high windows and dust sparkled in the air. Roosters perched on windowsills and chrome workspaces, bellowing their calls. I had no idea that chickens came in so many colours and shapes.

"Welcome to our chaotic home!" Sam announced with a broad grin. "Aren't they cute?"

The chaotic part certainly seemed accurate. The noise and dust were overwhelming. I sneezed into my FFP2 mask.

The Sanctuary, as it was known, was about an hour's walk from the park where I had met Sam and Heather that morning. From the outside, it was an imposing factory building with high fences and colossal doors that creaked as we entered through them. Just inside the entrance, through a series of smaller rooms, the three of us were taken through decontamination—to protect our friends, I was informed—and I got to take my first hot shower since I had left home. We were swabbed for various viruses and I got sterile booties to put over my trainers. We washed and disinfected our hands three times. I'm sure most people would hate it, but for me it felt comfortingly familiar.

Standing now in the main area, we were surrounded by hundreds of chickens perching and flying between pieces of factory equipment. A group of people passed by us with buckets full of chicken manure. *That must be a full-time job*, I reasoned. They opened a door to the outside and at least ten chickens bundled out with them in squawky disorder.

"That goes out to the yard," Sam told me. "We're just getting started and it's still a bit messy. But maybe it's less overwhelming for you?"

"Sounds good," I replied. Outside had to make more sense than this scene of mechanised industry overtaken by anarchic poultry. We followed the fluffy chicks and stepped through the door. A bit messy was an understatement.

The roofed yard of the factory was surrounded on all sides by fences and nets. The nets were clearly to keep the chickens separate from wild birds, but I couldn't escape the feeling that we were trapped inside a giant bag of oranges. Most of the yard was covered with straw where chickens pecked and scratched around for food and, every now and then, suddenly chased each other in circles.

One of the people carrying a bucket disappeared out through a net doorway.

"The poop has its own processing area out there," Sam explained. "Most of it is used as a kind of fertiliser out in the gardens. And here—" They led me to a corner of the yard. "Is where we have our compost."

Wooden pallets had been placed on their side creating a box. The pile of slimy, decomposing food inside was apparently very interesting to the chickens who gathered around to peck at the scraps and bugs. There were shreds of vegetable strewn everywhere. It wouldn't have taken much to come up with a better design, but the whole Sanctuary project seemed to me to be incomplete and disordered. I knew I should hate it; I didn't. A cautious mother chicken passed by, leading a line of fluffy chicks behind her.

Looking up, I saw that on the other side of the net, people were building a raised vegetable bed out of recovered materials. Others stood around a completed bed, tying string to a tripod of sticks. I had no idea what it was all about, but the cheerful busyness of the people and the intense energy of chickens was drawing me in. And most importantly, after so much time feeling threatened by every stranger who crossed my path, I was relieved to be around people who cared about chickens and vegetable beds.

"There's another section that used to be a public park out here," Sam told me. If we stay on the concrete, we won't need to go back through decontamination. Here I'll show you." They led me to the doorway in the net that the others had used. "Be careful that the chickens don't get out," they warned me as they unfastened the door, and we stepped carefully out into the park.

"Wow."

Sam smiled. "Right?"

Beyond the roofed yard, the sun was radiant, and the park buzzed with life. There was another ring of fence maybe twenty metres away. Within the fence, a lawn had become a spontaneous, richly entwined habitat of newly planted fruit trees and makeshift lean-tos. There were long white ducks swimming in a pond. A group of children sat in a circle in the grass, deep in a conversation that looked suspiciously like a meeting.

"It's incredible." I was genuinely impressed. "How long?"

"A year. More or less." Sam answered. "But me and Heather joined a week or so after things really fell apart, so three months ago."

"Only three months..." I said, trying to process that information.

"The fruit trees went in last week. We rescued them from a burned-out gardening centre. The ducks arrived by themselves a few days ago, I guess from some farm somewhere. They've been laying eggs under the bushes. And the chickens have all been rescued from industrial farms or were found abandoned in private yards."

"And the flu?"

"We're doing everything we can," they said, indicating the net fence. "But it will come. And then we'll have to make some difficult decisions. For now, they had to go somewhere, and we love them. Luckily, we have a couple of vets in the network who come every week to take swabs and check on our friends. It's all we can do for now."

"And how does it all work?" I asked, looking around. "Is this place open to anyone? How do you decide who can join and stay here?"

"Have you heard of the Imperative?"

I shook my head. "Like a biological imperative?" I asked.

"Maybe. We're still working it out—what it is and what it means." Sam gave me a knowing look. "But if you were trying to ask if you can stay here then the answer is yes. Me and Heather have already vouched for you, and we were out this morning specifically looking for people we thought might be…you know.”

“Changing?”

“Exactly.”

I was surprised. “But we’ve known each other, what, six hours?”

“We seem to recognise each other, instinctually somehow. But nothing is certain at this point.” Sam looked thoughtful as they turned back towards the factory building. “And anyway, biology doesn’t guarantee anything. You’ll need to go through a process—some trainings and workshops. We all did them. We’re trying to keep things as safe as—”

In that moment, a particularly fluffy grey chicken with black spots and a little feathery crest on her head came up to the other side of the net fence and squeaked at us.

“Oh hello!” Sam said in a joyful voice. “Brook, let me introduce you to someone.”

Sam led me back through into the yard. They bent down and picked the chicken up. “This is Gerbil. She was one of the first to be born here.”

“Erm…” I said, having never been introduced to a chicken before. “Hi?”

Sam grinned, “Here, put out your hands.” They plopped Gerbil into my forearms. She nearly fell, flapped her wings to stabilise and I got a face full of chicken dust. “Support her feet with your hands…that’s right. There, she’s comfortable now.”

And I could see that she was. She lay herself down on the little platform of my hands. Her belly feathers were fluffy and warm, her scaly little legs were relaxed on my skin and, just like that, she closed her eyes and went to sleep.

“She likes you,” Sam said.

“Wow,” I repeated. My first time cuddling a chicken, my first time in a squatted factory, and my first glimpse of what the Shift might mean for the world. It was a big day.

The guided tour of the Sanctuary turned into lunch around plastic tables in the yard. Although I was quiet, the others around my table seemed friendly. They didn't ask me too many questions, which I appreciated. Sam and I spent the rest of the afternoon scrubbing chicken roosts and collecting eggs. Dinner and bedtime soon followed.

It wasn't a hard decision to stay. I had never lived communally before, but anything had to be better than another night trying to sleep in a park. Sam took me out into the yard; empty now that the chickens were all sleeping inside. We came to a winding staircase that led up to the first floor.

"Downstairs, as you probably saw, was all the factory floor," they explained as we started up the stairs. "Upstairs was the office area. The staircase was built outside so that the white-collar workers never had to mingle with the people downstairs although they all worked for the same company. Classed architecture, I guess."

"Makes sense," I said. "Did any of the workers join the occupation?"

Sam paused and looked back down at me. "A few. The office people were all long gone by the time I got here but about a dozen of the factory workers came back and joined the collective. They were very cautious to begin with. They didn't trust us one bit."

We both reached the top of the stairs.

"I can understand that," I said. "What convinced them to stay, do you think?"

"I think they just had no choice. No-one was really getting by out in the world. And the Sanctuary is all about meeting material needs. No flags. No documentaries. Just food and shelter and maybe a bit of community if we're lucky."

I nodded. I wasn't very experienced in activist culture but compared to that one long, hungry meeting before I met Cooper, the Sanctuary seemed like another world. I like to say that I can smell pretention a mile away and this project already felt much more grounded.

"'Working together to meet our needs,' is how we describe it." Sam's voice held a touch of pride. "It's almost become a slogan or something. Sorry, I know that's really wanky."

I smiled. "I like it."

"Me too," Sam's expression grew serious. "Honestly though, it's also a lot sometimes."

They looked down over the yard. "Some of us had experience of this kind of organising before—Heather has been active for most of her life. But for me, this is all new. I'm glad we have that history of organising to draw on and we're not alone—this is all just one small part of a movement. But sometimes I still feel lost. I guess we're just all just learning as we go. And trying to keep up."

I listened patiently. "It sounds like a lot. But it seems like you're also doing amazing work here."

Sam gave me a gentle smile, "Thank you. I think I'm just tired. Ready to go in? We'll need to be quiet."

I nodded and Sam opened the door. We stepped silently into the bedroom.

Perhaps fifty mattresses were scattered on the floor amongst potted rubber plants and water coolers. Desks were stacked up along the walls. Although the sun had only just set, most of the mattresses were already full of people sleeping and snoring. *Living on chicken time,* I noted to myself.

Silently, Sam showed me to an empty mattress, already made up with a pillow and duvet.

"In case you need anything, Heather is over there—" they whispered, pointing to where their friend was sleeping near a pile of computer equipment. "I have a night shift on security, so I'll see you in the afternoon some time. Sleep well and... welcome."

Despite the sounds and smells of people sleeping all around me, despite the weirdness of being in a new place I barely understood, I was out within seconds. I slept uninterrupted until lunchtime.

* * *

I woke up feeling refreshed and excited by possibilities. Heather spotted me as I made my way down the staircase and waved me over to join her at a picnic table in the yard.

"I saved you some breakfast," she announced. People shuffled up the bench to make space for me to sit.

"Thank you, I appreciate it."

Heather nodded. "That's the last of the gluten-free bread and honey. We get them from another collective across town. I'll be heading over there soon."

"Can I join you?" I asked. The Sanctuary felt comfortable, and I wasn't particularly anxious to be back outside the gates. But I *was* curious. There were other collectives. How far did this new world extend?

"Sure. The more the merrier."

We headed out soon after.

* * *

The city I had known for the best part of a decade had been transformed in a matter of months. Passing through whole neighbourhoods on our bikes gave me an overview I had been missing on foot. Roads were lined with piles of stinking garbage. A queue of abandoned cars snaked out of a smashed-up petrol station. A whole tower building seemed to have been burned, smoke still billowing out of the top floors. And in between the devastation, signs of hope in the projects we visited.

The first, a squatted cinema, now community bakery. Bread was distributed out of the old ticket booth and people chatted to each other in the queue, washed over by waves of warm baking smells. Heather led me to the back of the building where four newly built brick ovens in the yard were attended by a group of busy people.

Someone wearing a flour-covered apron came over to greet us. "Hey Heather. How is it? Got some eggs for us?"

She pulled four big boxes out of her backpack and handed them over.

"Duck eggs too this time. No idea where they came from, but they're laying like it's the end of the world."

The baker smiled warmly. "Great, we'll use those for the pastry glazes. Any sweets for the Sanctuary today?"

"Just bread will be fine," Heather replied. "Don't want people getting too comfortable."

The baker put four large loaves into a bag for us, then they gave me a wink and slipped in half a dozen cupcakes.

We set off again and my bag was already heavier than I expected.

Next, Heather brought us to what looked like a residential building. We stood at the door while she rang the bell three times. I saw someone on the ground floor peek through a drawn curtain. Soon after, the door latch was released, and Heather pushed it open.

The dark foyer beyond was cold and empty of people. In the centre of the tiled floor lay a bag of mixed vegetables and two dispensers of hand sanitiser. Heather put the supplies in her bag and instructed me to leave three boxes of eggs. We stepped back outside, and the warmth of the street was a relief.

"What's that place about?" I asked as we got back on our bikes.

"Not all the projects are closely aligned," she explained as we cycled down the street together. "Project 14, the cinema-bakery, are our friends and they've joined us for some meals. We helped them build one of the ovens, which was cool. But this place," she cast a glance behind us. "I don't think it has a name. They're only interested in exchange. I don't even know where they get the vegetables, and we don't ask. They're pretty grumpy... and that's me saying that, so you can imagine."

I laughed. I was getting to like Heather more all the time.

After a short cycle she signalled for us to stop by the side of a canal.

"We've earned ourselves a drink of water," she declared. "No point going back too early, we'll just end up in a meeting if we do."

We sat and watched the water passing by quietly as we sipped from our bottles. Although I didn't recognise the neighbourhood, I knew the canal was the same one that I used to walk along with Adam, glued to his phone, while I chatted away about sparrows. *How quickly things can change.*

* * *

That afternoon I sat with Heather and Sam on a straw bale inside the Sanctuary. Chickens ran around our feet and groups of people busied around with their tasks. We had just had a late lunch. It was good, but not everyone had had a full portion. With so many mouths to feed under one roof, it seemed that getting enough food was a challenge, even with all the connections to other projects. *And one more mouth just arrived yesterday,* I thought to myself. I internally committed to keep working hard to earn my keep.

I turned to Sam and Heather and asked, "How many projects is the Sanctuary working with? I know of two now, but I guess there's a lot more."

"It's complicated," Heather replied immediately. "As far as we know, there are lots of different ones, mostly food, textiles but also other things. There's a squatted bus line and even a hotel, although who's taking holidays these days is beyond me. We work with about twenty projects. There's a lot of conflicts to work through. A lot of negotiation and—as you've noticed—a great fondness for meetings."

I smiled. Although I'd managed to avoid them so far, there seemed to be a meeting, and working group, for everything in the Sanctuary.

"It makes sense that there are challenges," Sam added. "It's hard to agree about how to build this new world we're dreaming of."

"Project 18, for example," said Heather with a heavy tone. "I don't know if it will even make it through the first year."

"Project 18?" I asked.

"An occupied factory," Sam explained. "But not like here—they keep the actual factory running. They make linen, clothes, towels, all of that stuff, which is obviously unusual, as most of that got outsourced to the global south. And also really useful right now. Anyway, they drove the owners out and became a workers' owned co-op, but power for the machines is becoming less and less reliable."

"And they're running out of raw materials," Heather added. "We colonised the world with cotton. We made sweaters out of fossil fuels. And now we damn well need to work out some alternatives before the winter comes."

"There's a new project across the river that's working on flax," said Sam hopefully. "Maybe that will turn into something."

"Yeah, well let's see." Heather was hunched over. She had pulled a piece of straw out of the bale and was breaking it into ever smaller pieces.

"Well, *I'm* hoping it works out." Sam pushed their shoulders back.

"I am too, of course." Heather took another piece of straw. "I'm just not convinced that we can make *everything* we need to survive. Some people aren't getting their medications regularly enough. What happens when our stocks run out? As far as I know there are no pharmaceutical factories lying around waiting to be taken over."

"We never thought it would be easy. Or quick." Sam sounded defensive. "Transitions take time. But the Imperative exists now. We all feel it and we can't continue like we did before."

Already in the day and half since arriving at the Sanctuary, I had heard several people mention the Imperative. There were hearty conversations over mealtimes about what was happening to us. Some were calling it 'the Shift', as in a changing of paradigms. It seemed too grand a word for me, but I couldn't deny that something was changing. I listened on, ready to learn more.

"*Some of us* feel it for sure. But we have no way to know if everyone is changing like we are. Or what any of it means, honestly."

"That's true…"

"You're right though that we can't go on like we did before." Heather crossed her arms. "The system has gone, or at least a lot of it has. Somehow it was all a lot more fragile than we imagined. And when things don't magically appear in the supermarket or pharmacy, most of us haven't the first idea how to replace them."

"I know," Sam continued. "I see that. Somehow, Imperative or no Imperative, it's hard to believe we were *ever* a part of all that. How did we think it was okay to get our food from across the world and drive our cars to offices every day?"

"Yes, but also, what other options were there?" Heather sat up straight now, her eyes locked onto Sam's. "We grew up in a system that gave us no alternatives…by design. Supermarkets. Sweatshop clothes. There were no ethics; it was all bad."

"I'm just saying. Since the Shift, things are different. We can't ignore the bad things anymore."

"My mum was a nurse and dad worked in a call centre." Heather's voice was raised now. "We didn't have time to think about saving the climate, or the whales. We were focused on just getting to the end of the month."

Sam raised their palms in defence. "I'm sorry. I know. I didn't mean that, it's just…" They looked out over the factory floor where chickens were beginning to gather in corners to roost. "I'm just worried, I think. This isn't the first day we've run out of food before everyone was fed. As you say, we're running out of meds too. Antiretrovirals. Insulin. I feel like we're doing the best we can, but even with all our good intentions, I don't know how we're going to make it."

"You're right," said Heather, uncrossing her arms. "It's a fucking mess."

I absorbed the conversation but didn't join it. Although they were both tense, it was clear to me that they both agreed with each other—there were just so many feelings to process.

We had been born into a system of exploitation that could no longer exist and although the Shift had brought us a new sensitivity to the world, and to each other, we had a lot of unlearning to do before anything would really work again.

I also have to confess; I was really enjoying listening in. I felt stimulated, but comfortable. Maybe even a little bit at home. Gerbil was pecking around my feet, and I moved down onto the ground next to her. She climbed onto my lap and I scratched the back of her neck. I leaned my back against the straw bale and closed my eyes. The food in my belly, the warmth of Gerbil's little body, the voices around me, it all pulled me down into sleep and into gentle dreams of container ships and gulls soaring above a sun-lit ocean.

after

I awoke again, inside my cave, entangled in my torn and damp sleeping bag. The sun was streaming in on my face, strong and bright. My arms ached and my neck was stiff; I was exhausted. I had been dreaming again and it had all seemed so real. I rubbed the sleep from my eyes and stumbled outside into the afternoon light.

I walked out onto the beach. Trying to get my memories into some order, I noticed the strangest pain radiating from my sacrum. My tailbone.

I lost a tail feather in the fall. The air is never the same twice.

I faced the waves, my thoughts a jumble, when a familiar buzz ran down my spine. I turned on instinct. Laguna was making her way down the cliff side towards me. She wore an unusual brown dress, darker at the back than the front. Like a sky-circler. She carried a full backpack, a coil of wire over her shoulder, and a basketful of eggs. She was beautiful.

She arrived outside my cave and smiled.

My voice was more confrontational than I wanted it to be. "Is any of it real?" I demanded. "Did we fly?"

She took her time answering. She sat on the sand, cracked a boiled egg on a rock and began peeling away the shell. "Yes, it's real."

My heart jumped.

"More or less."

I watched her, mesmerised by her hands as they worked the eggshell.

"Sit with me, I'll explain what I can."

I sat.

"Have you noticed that time means something else when we're flying?" she asked me. I nodded before I had really thought it through.

On reflection, I had little sense of time in those days. My life had become circular—days and nights, the changing moon and the seasons fading into each other were the only meaningful measurements, and I had few ways to mark any of them. I was fairly sure I'd woken up in my cave twice since leaving the village. But the memories of learning to fly and hunt felt like they spanned a month at least. Both of those things couldn't be true, could they?

"It's okay. That's part of it."

Laguna bit into her egg, and I took one as well from the basket. I had to crack it in three different places and made a spider's web of tiny cracks. It took a while before it was free of shell and the task kept me occupied while I processed Laguna's words. I felt like we'd talked about this already, but maybe that was only in our other forms.

If that ever really happened.

I was overwhelmed and ate without tasting.

"I'm... I...don't really understand what's happening to me," I admitted, as I carefully avoided her eyes and reached for a slice of bread.

"I know, I'm sorry. What do you remember?"

I looked up. "We...flew together?" I felt ridiculous just saying the words.

Laguna nodded. "We did."

"And I crashed into a tree."

She smiled. "Actually, that's happened a few times but you're getting better at it. You're learning much faster than I did."

"Really?"

"I didn't have a teacher, I guess."

"And Aleena?"

"She only flew with me the first time. We drifted apart. Life got in the way."

My head filled with other questions.

"Is it real?" I felt my cheeks flushing. I was repeating myself, but I still needed to know.

Laguna took my hand in hers. It was dry and soft and perfect. "It's real enough. The time confusion only happens at the beginning while you're trying to process the new way of being. For me it lasted the first flight or two, and then things started to make more sense. It will pass."

"Is it... a trans thing?"

Laguna smiled. "It would be a cute metaphor, but no. I thought the same thing at first as well, but Aleena didn't seem to think it was connected. Or maybe a bit, I'm not sure."

"Okay," I said, not knowing what else to say.

"Just as there were many ways to shift, there are many ways to bridge. That's all I know."

I sat quietly, absorbing, and assimilating.

"And although it feels like it, our human bodies aren't really changing form. Each time we've met, you've been here—" she indicated the beach and my cave with her free hand. "And I've been in the village."

I looked at her, trying to understand.

"We... well, I don't know if *project* is the right word," she continued. "In my mind, I've always called it *expressing*."

"I love that."

"So okay, we *express* in our other forms, but our human forms remain too, in a kind of sleep wherever we are. Which is why bird-people don't really recognise us. We're not part of their society; we're just visitors."

"But we hunted," I offered. "And my tail hurts from the crash." I indicated my spine.

Laguna squeezed my hand. "Because it's real. Even if it's a kind of reality you're not used to yet."

I still couldn't understand.

"And that day—you flew into the cave but came out, as you, as human. And after the crash, you rubbed my head in the ferns..." I felt ridiculous, but I had no other way to put my thoughts together.

"I know, it's disorientating. How can I explain it?" Laguna looked thoughtful. "We recognise each other, whatever form we're in. And this has been the only way for your nervous system to process it until now."

"Okay..."

"You met my shadow-circler expression and you saw me. Both the human and the bird exist at the same time—and both are me. But I haven't been here in human form, since... well, since the night of the storm actually."

My stomach dropped.

"It will make more sense soon, I promise," Laguna said softly.

"And can we... express... whenever we want to?"

"More or less." Laguna released my hand. "When you've eaten, we can go again if you like."

I gulped down my food and pulled myself to standing. "Yes."

∗ ∗ ∗

"So, first we should make somewhere comfortable for us to lie down," Laguna suggested as we entered my cave. "Is this where you've been sleeping?"

I looked at my sad mess of a sleeping bag. "I used to have a mattress of ferns too, but..."

"—the storm."

"Yeah."

"Then let's make you a new one," Laguna said brightly. "It won't take long, and we'll still have time after that. Or we could even fly at night, we haven't done that yet, it's special... different."

Secretly I didn't want to wait, but it would be good to have help setting up my bed again. I didn't remember much from the last nights, but the sand had to be cold and hard.

"Let's do it."

I took Laguna to the bottom of the cliff and warned her about the unstable spot where I had once twisted my ankle. We climbed carefully and arrived quickly to the top. The last time we had made the climb together, Laguna had been injured and had needed to lean on me the whole way. I'm not sure how we made it up, it was steep.

I pushed the thought away. The idea of me hurting her seemed so alien, so unreal, I wanted to believe that it never happened. It would be much easier to never think of it again.

We stepped into the thicket of ferns that lined the cliff, and Laguna pulled out a pocketknife. My knife had probably been taken by the storm. I needed to do a full inventory of what was left and for a moment couldn't believe I hadn't done it yet. *I've been distracted*, I realised. And I was surprisingly okay with it.

"Are these the ones you use?" she asked me, cutting a large frond of fern. There was something about the sight of her there, surrounded by lush plant growth in every direction, the evening sun bright in her eyes that made me overly aware of my heartbeat. My ears were ringing. Maybe it was the experiences we'd been sharing over the last days and maybe it was my heart giving into the inevitable. I had the sense of being at the edge of something and I was both terrified and thrilled.

"Brook?"

"Sorry, yes. Any of the bracken will do." Then for whatever reason, I started babbling.

"Making bedding out of bracken was once pretty common practice. Especially before enclosure stopped people from accessing the land. It's nothing like the beds in the village, of course, but I find it's comfortable enough. One time I even threw in some eucalyptus leaves. I think it helps to keep the bugs away, but it also just smells really nice? Clean, I guess."

What am I talking about? No-one cares. And yet Laguna looked at me, her face soft and her eyes bright.

"You're sweet," she said.

My heart was pounding now.

"Thank you," I managed.

"Can I kiss you?"

The world blurred suddenly into disconnected perceptions. The coppers and spirals of the bracken in Laguna's hand. The vibrations of waves crashing below us. And most striking of all, a nightingale, a hundred metres away at the edge of the forest, singing his heart out. I narrowed in on that sound and it enthralled me.

People have obsessed over nightingales for centuries, projecting onto them symbols of love, or poetry, but in that moment, all I heard was sex. I was consumed by this little flycatcher pushing his honey song out into the world, no matter the expense. A song that had taken years to master and precious energy to produce. Music that had evolved to seduce its listeners; a vocal invitation to join him in a moment of fleeting pleasure. It was the most erotic sound I had ever heard.

I'll never know if he found a mate that evening. His sensual song would be drowned out by our cadenced moans of pleasure. For deep in the dark green of ferns and mosses, Laguna and I became entangled.

Together, we lost fear and separation. There was Laguna and there was me, but there were also our micro-communities intermixing through skin contact and saliva. There was the exploding richness of soil beneath us and the intoxicating pollen-air in our lungs.

My hands digging into the dirt, my arm kissed by nettles. A pair of blue dragonflies pausing on Laguna's naked back, resting together in exhausting embrace.

Our bodies created new, startling forms of connection. We knew traditional modes of intimacy would never be available to us—and that opened a world larger and richer than I could have hoped.

Like the fractal bracken, our orgasms spiralled and forced us outside. The sun burned the sky the deepest of reds and grip-releases and pleasure-waves ungrounded us for terrifying moments of aerial bliss. We were dusted in soil, and we were pulled earthwards.

By the time we made our way slowly down to the beach, night had fallen. The stars glistened anew. Even the crescent moon seemed to wink at us. They had seen it all, and we walked hand in hand through the surf, unashamed.

* * *

Just as Laguna had indicated, the confusion and time dilation stopped shortly after that. Time spent in our other forms began to match my regular time. Or at least a day was a day, and a night was a night, no matter what form I was in. I can't say it was exactly the same, because all my perceptions were so different, but it was beginning to make more sense.

After a restful morning by the water, we spent the afternoon exploring the beach. We had barely slept, but I felt full of energy and vast distances disappeared beneath our wings. I saw parts of the coast I had never visited before. A chalk headland carpeted with heath and shrubs and buffeted by gales and saltwater. A protected cove with still waters and smooth air that smelled like warm sand. I even got up the courage to fly out a short way over the water. Watching from above as dolphins swam and played below us, was a thrill like no other.

What we had shared in the ferns only made our flight more united. I could read every adjustment in Laguna's wings and knew when a gust of wind was coming towards me. She could tell by the way I spread my tail feathers that I was ready to rest in a hover and she joined me, soaring around in circles as the sun warmed our feathered bodies.

We were so different in our patterns, our muscles and nerves and senses all evolved for different ways of living, but we found a common place together in the air and the expression I found flying with Laguna felt like liberation.

As the sun moved closer to the horizon, we returned to my cave, and, for the first time, I fully remembered shifting back from my avian form. One moment we stood on the beach, our talons in the sand, making the decision.

The next, we were lying naked next to each other between ferns and the warm sleeping bag.

I kept my eyes tightly closed. Just like the transition from deep sleep, I needed time to adjust, to assimilate. Then slowly I opened them and took in the reds and oranges of the cave walls. Laguna was propped up on one elbow waiting for me.

She stood slowly, and her body was magnificent as she pulled on her underwear and slipped into the strange brown dress. She stepped a few metres over to her backpack and began arranging tools and strands of wire and pieces of wood.

"We have an hour or so before dark. I figured you might want some help rebuilding your shelves." She paused and looked at me, her eyes soft in the glowing light. "I know how you like to keep things tidy."

My heart burst then. Metaphorically of course, but the expanding warmth in my chest was real enough. I have never been more in love with anyone than I was in that moment.

during

The assistant to the billionaires tried the comm for the nineteenth time that day. Still nothing, not even static. Mission control had gone silent. A Florida hurricane, a terrorist attack, an invasion of killer alligators. Images of disasters flashed through her mind as she tried to control her ragged breathing. In the twelve years she'd been taking orbital flights, nothing like this had ever happened and she had no idea what else to do. Protocol was clear on the matter: no re-entry was possible without instructions from base. Theoretically, she could bring the shuttle back down by herself, but landing would be another matter entirely.

She was acutely aware that time was already up. Space pleasure cruises like this didn't come with weeks of extra fuel or the possibility of extending the trip. They were already two days over schedule and the four absurdly rich men in the living space behind her were champing at the bit. Over the last week, she had endured abusive insults and constant condescension. She hadn't signed up for this.

This wasn't her fault, she had explained. They just needed to wait for someone to respond. But patience wasn't a virtue for those who ran empires.

She already knew that no-one was going to help them get home. The image that now filled her mind was much more terrifying. An empty control centre. Monitors flickering in a room, the overhead lights still on. In her heart, she knew the hundreds of people it took to run the station had simply walked out, leaving them to their fate.

She almost didn't blame them. The men arguing on the other side of the hatch had plunged millions into poverty. They spent their wealth taking these trips just for the chance to look down on the planet they were murdering with oil and technology. They felt like gods up here, but they were the gods of destruction, and the assistant hated them as deeply as one human can hate another.

She tried the comm one more time and the silence steeled her for what was to come next. She pushed her shoulders back and released the strap holding her to the seat. Her diplomatic smile was tight and forced as she pushed herself through into the living room. The floating billionaires began their screaming accusations before she even closed the hatch.

They called her 'girl' even though she was nearly forty. She assured them that it was all okay, that she had finally made contact and there was some kind of glitch with the comms. She just needed to make a few last-minute checks—could they kindly prepare for re-entry?

She helped them back into their seats and attached their harnesses. They were so awkward in zero gravity and held her personally responsible for it.

You didn't need to come here, she thought to herself. No-one cared if you did.

Strapped into their chairs, their puffed chests and flushed faces still spoke of danger. The assistant left them there as she pushed herself through a corridor tube and arrived within seconds at the escape pod. There was space for two people in the pod, but she knew the billionaires would sooner kill her than let her negotiate a passenger. Or they would kill each other trying to decide who was important enough to be saved.

Her fingers ran quickly over the glowing buttons; putting to action the launch sequence she had been visualising on a loop for the last few hours. She knew that they had no idea what she was doing. They barely understood how their espresso machines worked, much less a space shuttle.

As she completed the sequence of actions that would take her back to Earth and strapped herself in, she knew her chances of survival would be low. Re-entry without guidance from control had its risks, even with all the automation. After she touched down in the Pacific Ocean, would anyone find her? How many weeks would she be floating there? How long would her water last?

No choice, she decided. The pod left with a hiss and a mechanical clunk of disconnection, pushing out into space.

The men knew nothing. They stared out of the portal at the stars, waiting impatiently for her return. The assistant navigated the pod behind the stern of the shuttle, engaged auto-pilot, and headed down towards the clouds. She didn't even think about looking back.

* * *

Sam caught their breath and smiled. "Thanks for letting me read today. That was fun!"

At the Sanctuary, stories like this were our equivalent of watching a movie together. We were gathered upstairs by candlelight, mattresses arranged in a circle. Sam had seemed full of life as they read from the book, hands energetic, eyes bright with details.

The escape was very welcome. This must have been day eight or nine since I arrived. Although I was feeling increasingly at home at the Sanctuary, our days were busy, meetings were long and tense. This time I had been one of those who didn't get enough food.

The Sanctuary had been abuzz since morning. We were expecting to host upwards of a hundred people the next day from aligned projects in the city. I had hand-washed dozens of towels and pillowcases, and my hands were wrinkly and sore. As Heather had described it, the gathering was intended to be partly a skill-share for crisis-survival, and partly a way to build social bonds. Which, as she put it, might be the most meaningful crisis preparation there is.

I was tired and hungry but also excited. Each day I realised more how much I had to learn; how interdependent our survival was. And I was beginning to have a sense that we were living through an important moment. That we could do a lot together. The world was feeling full of potential and possibilities.

No-one has ever accused me of being an optimist, but looking back on those moments now, I see how naïve we really were.

after

It was early morning and the sky was cloudy, the water rougher than usual. Ribbons of mist lay over the beach as Laguna and I took flight. She had spent the night again. I'm not sure if we slept. Perhaps a few restful moments were snatched between the hours of intensity. My cave walls could echo; I didn't know that before.

We began our flight over the cove where we had seen dolphins. I hoped to see them again, or even a migrating whale. Waves smacked loudly against the sand and a cold breeze was blowing. No dolphins. And the weather was changing. Without words, Laguna turned to fly inland.

I followed her, of course. Some part of me thought that we might be going to visit the village. Maybe I even *hoped* that we would.

I was curious. Was the fence still standing? Had the night-dogs come again? I could have easily asked Laguna, but somehow it didn't feel right. I was convinced that being back home was where I wanted to be and confessing that I thought about the village at all might leave me vulnerable.

The mist seemed to be following us inland and was thickening into a heavy fog. By my estimate of how far we'd travelled, and our distance from the hill and the marshland, we had arrived in the general area of the village. Below us we saw only white cloud.

I was reminded of a flight I'd taken once over London—when planes and holidays were still a thing. I was young and had been excited to get a window seat. I was ready to enjoy the view. The entire journey had turned out to be just variations on white and grey. I felt something like that disappointment as we flew past the invisible village.

Then I remembered how very different it was to be flying under my own power. How new and incredible it all was. It amazes me sometimes how quickly we become desensitised to the best things in life. It's sad too. I adjusted my wings and flew upwards to join Laguna.

From up high, the view was about the same, but the air was more bracing. We continued for a while, Laguna soaring forwards and my wings flapping hard to keep up. *We are built so differently. And I love that.*

Then, as if manifested from my distant memories of holidays, the cloud cleared a little and I saw that we were over the airport.

A small flock of pigeons on the roof reacted immediately to our presence and ducked down deeper into the fog. *So* that's *why we came*, I realised. *Breakfast.*

* * *

"We'll stay on the roof for a while," she explained. My brain was now used to the pitch of her sky-circler voice. "If we're patient, the pigeons will forget about us."

"Is it really possible to catch them?" I asked.

"The fledglings are the easiest." Her tone was serious and respectful.

We made our descent. Laguna perched near the edge, and I joined her. Close enough to get the best possible view, but far enough in, to hide our silhouettes. We waited with the infinite stealth of hunters; our bodies still and our senses attuned.

Above us, the overcast sky grew darker although it could only have been around midday. We were surrounded by fog on all sides, and I started to feel the itch of impatience. My wings ached with the desire to fly; to explore our territory, or at least to stretch a bit. But Laguna remained motionless.

Then, a new breeze arrived, and the fog started breaking up into patches. Small areas of the runway became visible before disappearing again. I caught a brief glimpse of the tail of a plane appearing like a whale breaching the ocean surface before it was swallowed by the fog. My hopes for a good meal were growing, and my mouth watered, but I was beginning to notice something in the air. Something wasn't right.

I caught Laguna's bright eyes and saw that she sensed it too. There was a new scent, something stinging and caustic that felt deeply wrong to our sensitive bodies. The breeze blew an opening in the fog, and we understood for the first time the danger we were in. The earthquake at the airport had only been the beginning. I stepped back in surprise and tried to take in the scene below us.

The thinning fog revealed concrete cracked open by the tremors. Oil and chemicals leaking out of the ground that formed a black river moving as slowly as lava. And just as deadly.

Under the airport lay massive containers of fossil fuels, anti-freeze, all the chemicals that once formed part of the airline industry. All exposed now by the shaking earth.

Oil had pooled on the asphalt creating a glossy black lake. Noxious chemicals distorted the air above and my eyes began to burn. The fog continued to clear, and we could see further along the runway. There, the oil-lake broke out into a multitude of streams. The poisonous rivers were heading out, away from the airport. Out into the marshlands. Out towards the village.

The terror that ran through Laguna's feathered body was as real to me as my own.

during

I woke up with a start; Sam was touching my arm. Their warm smile quickly soothed my panic and in silence we tidied away our mattresses and sheets, careful not to wake the others who were still sleeping. We slipped out of the bedroom and made our way carefully down the staircase to the yard. The morning was foggy and cool. I pulled open the chickens' door, and they exploded outside in their usual joyful chaos. It seemed that no matter how early we woke up, they were always waiting impatiently to be let out. They had no interest in being cooped up while there were worms to catch and straw to scratch around in.

We stepped inside and piled up cartons of eggs, collected the evening before. It was our turn to make deliveries, so we placed the cartons into our backpacks and the baskets of our bikes and made our way to the main entrance.

Leaving the Sanctuary was always a dramatic moment; the huge factory doors creaking open, morning light pouring in. Pushing my bike, and body, across the boundary between inside and outside, safety and the unknown.

We pulled the doors closed again and paused for a moment in the driveway outside. From here, no-one could guess at the life that was taking place behind these walls. I was fast becoming part of this hectic place of humans and birds. Maybe it was the experience of having nothing to call home for a while, or maybe it was this so-called Imperative that kept coming up in conversation—a mysterious force giving us the courage to come together and create something new. I couldn't say. But I was changing; we all were.

We stepped up onto our bikes and cycled out into the fog.

‚ ‚ ‚

* * *

A few hours later, our bikes and backpacks were heavy with vegetables and other essentials. My face was damp from the sun and the exercise. We had visited four different spaces in the neighbourhood, and I was more than ready for lunch.

The gathering would start in the afternoon and although participants were expected to bring food to share, we would still need a lot of supplies to feed all those people. More bike teams would set out soon, and I still doubted it would be enough.

We turned the corner and where the entrance to the Sanctuary was usually deceptively quiet, there was a mass of people gathered outside. The atmosphere was tight with stressed voices, exhaustion, and confusion. The noise was overwhelming.

Heather was off to the side in a heated discussion with a group of people. We pulled over next to her.

"What's happening here?" Sam asked.

Heather pulled away from the conversation and turned to us. Her eyes were wide.

"We're locked out." She pointed towards the doors, and I saw the heavy chains and locks.

"How?" I asked. "Who?"

"We think it was the original owners." Heather shook her head. "Someone came by after you both left and locked up the bottom floor. Most of us were still sleeping upstairs."

My heart dropped. "The chickens! Are they okay?"

Heather's expression changed. "They were locked in too. We cut through the park fence to get out. And a few people have gone to find bolt cutters to try the door. But the thing is, now people are scared. If they could do this, what else are they capable of?"

after

Danger. Perched above disaster, my thoughts came slowly as we took in the oil slick and its implications.

"We need to get to the village," I declared. Laguna showed her agreement in the way she shifted position of her feathered form. I imagined our human bodies lying next to each other in my cave.

"Should we stop expressing?" I asked. "And make our way there from the beach?"

"No," she said. "We're faster in the air."

"But how can we tell them? Who will understand us?"

Laguna had made her decision and didn't reply. She pushed off the roof of the airport building and took flight. I didn't understand but after the things we had shared—many of them mid-air—there was little room for doubt. I joined her in the sky. My mind focused in, and my body followed. I felt the wind and the power of my muscles as we moved quickly above the slicked runway and out over the land.

I flew with the kind of speed that comes from pure concentration. I ascended at a shallow angle until I'd reached enough height to drop again; my wings pulled back for extra velocity.

Laguna soared above me, so high I could barely see her through the clouds. Her larger, wider wings were perfect for harnessing the upper air currents to move faster. My smaller body, so well adapted for diving, was good at gaining speed lower to the ground. In this way, separately but together, we made our way towards the village at full speed.

We had travelled perhaps half the distance to the village when a sharp pain crashed down on my brain and my consciousness. It was so sudden, I gasped and dropped several metres before catching the wind. My vision on the left was filling with jagged lines. I wanted to throw up.

A migraine. Why now?

Then I saw them, the lightning flashes on the horizon, far out to sea. An electric storm was coming in fast.

"Laguna!" I called, but she was high above me, and I couldn't tell if she'd heard.

I inhaled deeply to try to call her again, but my brain was shutting down. Another cascade of pain and I closed my eyes. I fell fast.

during

We entered the Sanctuary yard through the park fence, and I was relieved to see that the chickens seemed to be fine, scratching and exploring as usual, unaware that anything had happened. Gerbil ran up to me, but I ignored her for now. I joined the stream of people making their way upstairs. It was a meeting I couldn't miss.

People arriving for the gathering also joined the assembly. The sleeping space-meeting room was already busier than I had ever seen it.

"We need to strike back!" Heather shouted. "If we let the fuckers get away with this, who knows what will be next?"

"Yes, it's terrible," said someone else. "But fighting the owners is just going to piss them off even more. We know they don't have... the Imperative, like we do. So anything is possible at this point."

"We don't actually know that for sure," said someone else.

"Why else would they act like this?"

"It doesn't matter," shouted Heather. "This is our home now, and we need to protect it!"

The meeting was fractious and panicked from the very beginning. New arrivals were constantly entering the room, and it was hard to keep the conversation on track. We were scared.

One group, including Sam, went off to start cooking. I sat in a corner, unsure where I could be most helpful. I certainly wasn't saying much in the meeting, and I knew nothing about tactics or defence strategies. I was about to get up to join Sam in the kitchen when I heard cries of alarm from the other end of the room.

"Gas!" someone shouted. "They're gassing us."

I smelt vinegar; my eyes burned. Tear gas filtered up through the floor. A window broke and a canister skidded across the room. The panic expanded and embraced us all and my senses seemed to shut down one by one.

after

My memory here is a bit fragmented.

After the ground speeding towards me, my next recollection was of Laguna sat nearby in my cave. I don't know how long I was out. We had stopped expressing, we were back in our human forms in the bed we had made together.

Laguna's face was filled with concern—and she made a gentle sound from deep in her throat. It was the sound that had brought me back. Then came waves of pain as I realised just how badly I was injured.

"Rest," she was telling me, and I had a memory of my tent in the village where she'd given the same order. "You fell. You're injured."

I tried to lift my head but could barely move.

"The oil!" I shouted, surprising myself with the strength of my own voice. "The village—we need to tell them!"

Laguna shook her head. "We can't—"

She nodded towards the cave entrance: the sky was strobing with lightning. There was no rain, but the flashes were constant. Slowly, coming back to alertness, I realised I'd been hearing the crashing storm for a while.

"We have to wait."

"I'm fine," I declared as I tried to sit up. Weakness and nausea passed through me, and I fell back down onto the bed. My head was pounding.

"No, Brook. We can't go anywhere until the weather clears."

I knew she was right, and my body begged for rest. But I also knew that an insidious enemy was leaking from the airport. The village—hell, the entire marshland—was in danger.

"How long?" I asked.

Laguna's expression was grave. "If it stays dry, maybe a day until the oil reaches the village. If it rains, then a lot less than that."

"And if lightning strikes in the wrong place—"

"—then there's not much we can do about it," she said finally. She stood and turned towards the newly rebuilt kitchen area of the cave. "I'll make us some food. Try to sleep."

I was awash with conflicting emotions and impulses to do something. Yet somehow Laguna's commands had the power to reach beyond my determination. Darkness closed in and I slept.

* * *

I woke a few hours later in the cave and knew straight away that my body wasn't right. I ached all over as I rolled onto my side. Apart from the pain itself, I was filled with frustration. There was an emergency to deal with and I was injured again. I felt betrayed by the fragility of my own body. My mind filled with images of lightning and burning rivers.

Laguna was nowhere to be seen, but when I called her name, she appeared within seconds at the opening of the cave. She carried a bowl full of seaweed and I could smell its salty, umami scent even from the bed. My senses were on hyperdrive, and the scent made me gag.

"How are you feeling?" she asked without preamble.

"Pretty rough," I had to admit. "I get migraines sometimes when the weather changes."

Laguna gave me a sympathetic look. "The lightning has let up and we need to get to the village." She stood abruptly. "Should I go without you?"

I knew my expression was pitiful, but I couldn't help myself.

She looked thoughtful. "Unless you can fly?"

My heart skipped. *Could I?* I was injured in my bird-form. Would the migraine follow me across the transition? *How does any of this work?*

Only one way to know.

"I can try," I replied.

I rolled onto my back and closed my eyes. I was vaguely aware of

Laguna tucking me into the sleeping bag. My body was warm and the bracken beneath me was soft until I lost all connection to that experience. The bed, and my mammalian breath, were gone. The pain in my back and skull was just a memory of a memory. I sat next to Laguna on a sentinel rock preening my feathers ready for flight.

"Well, hi," she said with a smile looking down at me. I stopped preening and looked straight at her. My instincts were telling me to move further away from this large being. To take flight and move to the air where I was safer. I fought my impulses and stayed. I knew her; this human was my home.

I released a high and short 'kee' from my beak and she seemed to understand.

"Good," she replied. "I'm glad you're feeling better."

We both looked over at the human resting at the back of the cave.

"Don't worry," Laguna explained to me. "You can come back anytime you need to." She stepped inside and lay the bowl of seaweed on a hanging shelf. "In case you get hungry."

I flapped my wings.

"Yes, we need to go." And so we left the cave. Laguna climbed the cliff quickly without hesitation and I hovered above her patiently. We passed through, and over, the field of bracken and across, and over, the land together. Our bodies were separated by hundreds of metres and three hundred million years of evolution, but we stayed synchronised. My flight call was a high yip-yip-yip-yip and each time, Laguna looked up to let me know she had heard.

Within an hour, we had reached the village.

It looked like a perfectly normal day in the community. A group of people were shovelling compost onto the vegetable beds and others were corralling a reluctant chicken back into her enclosure. The air smelled of drying herbs and new bread. They had no idea what was coming.

I hovered for a while then unconsciously moved higher. As if delaying the bad news might somehow make it untrue.

during

I'm not sure I can describe what happened at the Sanctuary on the day the owner and his private security arrived to evict us. And I'm not completely sure that I want to. The violence inflicted in those short, brutal hours was something new and unthinkable, until it became just another fragmented trauma-memory of one more home lost. A blanket of shock descended over us. We had to leave.

"I know a place we can go," said Heather as she, Sam and I stood in the park, surrounded by other Sanctuary members milling around, looking lost and terrified.

"Anywhere has to be better than here," Sam declared and rubbed their eyes on their sleeve. They hadn't stopped crying since carrying Gerbil's crushed body out of the Sanctuary. She was one of many who had been killed during the panic and it had taken all of Heather's negotiation skills to get permission from the security guards to re-enter the building to retrieve their bodies. We stood next to the grave we had dug our feathered friends and Sam continued to weep.

We collectively abandoned the building that same day and, as Heather led our group away into the city, not one of us could find the strength to look back. The guilt was overpowering.

∗ ∗ ∗

With Sam, Heather and three others, I moved to a squatted post office close to the canal. It was tight, uncomfortable living—our bedroom was in essence a single storage room with no windows—and without the rhythms of the Sanctuary, we were lost.

Two weeks passed in a blur. Sam fell into an all-consuming

depression and despair, and I slipped into a care role for them. Just making sure they ate enough and left the house at least once a day became my full-time job. I didn't choose the role, just as Sam didn't choose their breakdown. It just happened and we adapted quickly to this new normal.

On the other hand, I had never seen Heather more filled with energy. The eviction had galvanised her with a desire for revenge.

Downstairs, in the shop area where people had once queued to send parcels and buy stamps, crowds started to gather in the evenings. The meetings grew each day and from upstairs in our makeshift flat, as I prepared food over a camping stove and coaxed Sam to eat, we could hear the raised voices below.

Finally, on the seventh evening, my curiosity overcame my exhaustion, and I went downstairs to join the crowd gathered there. I was shocked to hear the action they were planning against the factory owners. I was even more surprised to find myself joining them a few days later.

<h1 style="text-align:center">after</h1>

As Laguna arrived in the village circle, people began descending from tree houses and making their way towards her.

Hovering above, I could hear the panic in their voices, see the physical tension moving through the group as Laguna explained the situation.

She paused for a moment and pointed at me. The others looked up and stared. But surely, they didn't understand who I was. *How could they? What is she telling them?*

The first drops of rain fell on my hovering body. There was no time to lose.

I flew higher and banked over the marsh towards the airport. I didn't need to fly for long before I could smell the hydrocarbons in the air. Even from above, my eyes began to sting and a few minutes later I could see the oil itself, smearing the stream with rainbows that could have been beautiful if they weren't harbingers of death.

The oil had reached halfway to the village—waterways were choked, grassy banks were smothered, and the marsh was turning into a toxic stew. It was so much worse than I could have imagined. The land was poisoned. Our habitat was dying.

during

Destruction, I've learned, can consume us like a fever. I resisted my desires for order and tidiness and allowed the infection to take hold. As I threw a second open pot of blue paint, I leaned into entropy.

"Is it enough?" I asked Heather. I saw in her bright eyes that the fever was taking her too.

"He took away our home, we'll ruin his," was her reply.

We had started with the bay windows, simple bricks thrown, almost iconic, through the glass. Others had gone behind the house to begin on the garden. I heard a loud splash as something heavy was pushed into the pool.

Around me, pots of paint, liberated from an abandoned hardware store, flew through the spaces left by the windows and even from outside, we could see the irreparable mess we'd made of the interior. I stared at my rainbow-coloured hands. Enough. None of this was particularly strategic; it was revenge through and through. We had come to manifest our anger at the factory owner and our message was unmistakable.

I knew deep down that he was rich enough to replace everything we had broken. Even if the industry which brought him such comfort and luxury no longer existed, he would continue to live an easy, protected life. Belonging to the owning class meant much more than just money and new furniture. But we had made our point. He'd be a bit less wealthy and feel less safe in his own home. And that was good enough for me.

I could already see smoke spiralling up from the back of the house and knew that none of this was even close to being finished. Our mob—let's not call it a demonstration—was still growing, and I realised in that moment that I needed to get out. I ignored Heather's confused shouting as I turned and left.

* * *

As I made my way up the stairs, my body was heavy with exhaustion and the sense of returning from a battle. My arms and legs were covered in paint.

I arrived back at our cramped home above the post office and found Sam, curled up asleep on their mattress. As usual. As far as I knew, they hadn't been out of the flat in days, maybe even a week. The plate of food I had made for them sat untouched on the desk where I'd left it.

Normally, this would have been enough to pull me in. My mind would have filled up with anxious thoughts of how I could be doing more to help them. My heart would beat faster, my body would get tight, and I'd have to replace the restlessness with action—probably cooking something else for them to poke at, or cleaning something that was already perfectly clean. Their depression was gravity, and I could barely resist.

But I was just too tired. I was so drained from the events at the owner's house that my body couldn't have generated panic, anxiety or worry, even if I wanted to. Instead, I collapsed onto my own mattress and slept right through to the next day.

* * *

I rubbed my eyes and sat up in bed, trying to clear my thoughts.

Heather stood in front of me, talking loudly about the action. She spoke so quickly I could barely follow. Sam lay near me on their mattress, their expression distant. They nodded vaguely, clutching a cup of coffee like their life depended on it.

"And that's when the owner came back—with his mates, I guess," Heather was saying, more animated than ever. Her voice was a harsh staccato. "Armed this time—though who knows if the guns were loaded. We were gone before we had to find out. Marj was stuck in the garden for a hot minute—we had to pull her over the fence. Her leg got all cut up..." She paused to take a breath then continued her frenzy of words. "Don't worry, she'll be okay. She's downstairs now. The meeting's about to start—I should go back down—it's going to be a big one."

Heather turned to me; her eyes were bright. "Shall we go down? You ready?"

She could have asked me if I was okay or why I'd left early. She could have worried that I didn't normally sleep fourteen hours straight. She could have shown more concern to Sam, who was fading away in front of our eyes.

But I didn't expect her to. In those days, so many of us were being called, and direct actions were as good a place to channel our feelings as any other. I also knew it made little difference. Either I'd be addicted to taking care of Sam and trying to save them from themself, or I'd join Heather in her equally powerful addiction to the fight. Either way, I was searching outside of myself for solutions and that never ends well for me.

I've gotten better at that. Living alone in a cave has given me plenty of opportunity to meet myself in all my naked vulnerability and to confront what I found there.

I've learned that I need to start where I have the most influence and to start with love—no matter how weak that sounds.

I've learned that some structures need dismantling, but if I dismantle myself and my marginalised body to get there, the powerful still end up winning.

I've learned that there are all kinds of roles for all kinds of people and not everyone needs to be on the front line.

But those lessons wouldn't come for a while yet. I went down the squeaky staircase and stepped into the main room to join the meeting. It felt like I was jumping into fast flowing water—the energy from those gathered was a physical and powerful thing. I allowed myself to be pulled under and carried along by the flow.

Heather spoke with determination and passion. The action at the owner's house was just the beginning. They would never let us build our new world, we had to take back the power.

We were going after the rich, the one percent, the billionaires, and nothing could stop us.

after

The rain was becoming a light drizzle. I made my way back to Laguna and cautiously landed on the damp grass.

She knelt down next to me. "Brook. How bad is it? Is the oil getting close?"

I ruffled my feathers and she understood.

"I need to stay here and help the others get organised." I remained still, listening to her strange mammal voice, somehow comprehending every word. "We'll try to divert the slick away from the village and block it from getting closer. But I don't know how much we can do without help."

I cocked my head.

"Are you okay?" she asked me. "Your other form, I mean."

I cast my mind to the cave. My sleep was restless and fevered. Pain still enveloped me.

I pulled back and nodded my feathered head.

"Okay good. Brook, we need to bring others to help. We can't do this alone."

I looked at her, unsure.

"You need to bring the other-people."

My mind filled with questions. *How could I communicate with them and how could they help?* Laguna had told me herself that even in this form, I wasn't really a part of wind-hover society. I felt helpless.

Laguna's serious expression broke into a gentle smile. "I know. It's a lot. You're used to thinking of yourself as an individual. But you're not and you never really have been. You're a whole community—let them speak, they know how."

I flapped my wings. I trusted her. It was Laguna after all, if she said I could bring the others, I would do my best.

"You should start in the forest," she nodded north, towards the mountains on the horizon. "Thank you, my love." She got up and turned back to the village.

* * *

I stood on the damp forest floor, my wings tucked, my feet gripping the soil with anxiety. Water dripped from leaves all around me. I had no idea what was supposed to happen next. Laguna had said I would understand how, but in that moment the future was a tangle of fruit and thorns and possibilities.

Lying in my cave, I could feel my migraine getting worse. I was becoming feverish, confused. My consciousness was spread between two bodies and in neither did I feel certain of myself.

In that moment, as if my mind was scanning for possibilities and solutions of how to communicate with the others, I flashed on thoughts of ecology: the study of home.

I thought about togetherness. Of species co-creating the world they need to live in. I thought of co-operation as an evolutionary strategy. Maybe, I reasoned, communication *was* possible because we had literally evolved to understand each other. We were all related, all connected. We shared ancestors and a planetary history.

But I'm a *predator*. Nature, red in tooth and claw. How many times had I fed with Laguna on the very creatures that I now hoped to speak with? And how many others would happily feed on me if they had the chance? Competition, struggle, and death. Survival of the fittest.

But that wasn't the whole story either. Life is neither competition nor cooperation; life is complexity.

I began to think about my human body, lying kilometres away. It was swirling inside with other cells. Back in my laboratory days, I remembered reading that bacteria and others, living in and on me, maybe even outnumbered my own human cells. And that felt right somehow. How much of me was even mammal?

And those human cells, didn't they each contain mitochondria, once independent micro-organisms who now gave me life? Where did *I* end and where did *other* begin?

The idea of Brook—an individual distinct from all others—meant nothing to the ecosystem I belonged to. Or to the community that dwelled inside me. I was multitudes and had always been.

And in that moment, as if my individuality itself was dissolving, life no longer felt linear. Time was a cycle that never ended, and we were all a part of it, interconnected and interexisting. We were inseparable—I was part of it and so were you. We still are.

As the birds and mammals, insects, amphibians, and reptiles began to gather around us and the trees and fungal networks themselves seemed to lean in, I told them my message. It came as a series of high, repetitive shrieks but they understood. We were in danger. We needed to act. And they agreed.

* * *

I flew back to the oil-slicked river, perched in a tree, and waited. Time had passed, that much I was certain of, but the sky was so dark. It could have been hours, it felt like minutes. The rain was much heavier now.

Had I been successful in my mission? What would success even look like?

My mammalian fever was spiralling, and I was losing my grip. The village was in danger, and I was helpless to stop it. Or I had done enough already. If the events in the forest had been true.

Then I saw the others arriving.

A black cloud of crows, jackdaws and ravens emerged from the wooded horizon. As their silhouettes grew closer, I could see that each one carried a branch in their beak. The cloud condensed, swirled, and descended over the water. A shower of twigs fell onto the slick, and from where I was perched, I could see the pile of wood building up and slowing the oil's insidious flow.

Next were the beavers, picking their way across the marshland, coming from all directions. I had no idea so many lived out here. Now the flow was slower, they got to work downstream, chewing through the trunks of narrow birch trees that lined the water. Within minutes, the first tree crashed down. With so many beavers cutting at once, the air filled with the sound of breaking wood and leafy branches hitting the water. Together they created a dam that filled twenty metres of the slowing stream.

Deer arrived, each dragging a heavy branch which, even from above, I could see was white with fungal rot. Gracefully and with care, the deer laid down their loads at the edge of oil-slicked water, cautious not to splash their sensitive muzzles. I knew, as they knew, that the fungal cells were ready to adapt and start breaking down the oil at impossible speeds. They knew, as I knew, that they had been preparing for this moment for generations.

But it still wouldn't be enough.

I flew downstream and saw that the villagers had also begun to divert the toxic tide.

This is sacred work, I thought to myself. This is how we show devotion.

At one point, over a million dams strangled Europe's waterways, making it the most dammed river landscape in the world. Unlike those concrete atrocities, the villagers were coming together to build a dam of straw and hay and sticks and piles of leaves stored since the autumn. This was a dam to *save* the river.

Some villagers pushed overladen wheelbarrows of materials to the water's edge while others built the structure itself. The surface movement of the stream was slowing, but there was still so much to do.

And we're nearly out of time, Laguna realised, as she looked towards the horizon.

Laguna stood on a platform between two huts to get an overview. Even from afar, she could perceive the oil's advance by the changing reflectivity of the water, the shimmering mirage of poisoned air, and the sharp toxic scent.

But wait. How can I...what's happening?

Despite the distance between us, Laguna saw me and for a moment I saw myself too. The arc of my talons wrapped around the branch. My feathered outline and the curve of my bill. My yellow-ringed eyes as black as night. Even given our discordant forms, we were connected.

"Are you okay?" she asked me. "I know this is a lot."

"I think so."

Laguna's tension was tangible to me. I felt her exhaustion being pushed away. Steadying her body weight, she put both hands on the railing. "I'm so proud of you."

She must have sensed my confusion because she followed up quickly with, "I knew you'd work it out."

"Have you done this before?" I asked her. "Communicated with the other-people?"

"We do it every day," she replied. "And they're always listening. You just found a way to focus that communication. Like I'm doing now."

I connected for a split second with my body, fevered and wracked with pain.

"But I'm not other-people!" I protested. *I'm there, in a cave, fully human.* "Am I?"

I physically felt her shrug her tired shoulders. "Is there a difference? Our words and binaries are always incomplete."

I didn't have time to understand. In that moment, despite the work of the beavers, crows and deer, the oil burst through our defences. There was just too much of it. It should have stayed in the ground.

The oil began to flow quickly once more towards the village and although a good amount of the poison had been absorbed by wood and branches, the movement was unstoppable.

I looked downstream back to where Laguna was still suspended in the trees. Only the human-made dam stood now between the oil and the village and there was nothing more we could do here. Chemicals began to overflow the banks of the river and the other-people scattered to safety.

Which, in the way that these things tend to happen, is when the lightning began again. And with deadly force, the air seemed to tear itself apart all around us.

* * *

The sky darkened as it filled with water.

Cumulonimbus dominated the west: a sheer cliff of cloud towering for miles, its anvil top whipped flat by storm winds. It was this single cloud, defined against the sunless sky, that produced the first strikes. Lightning spilled out from its dark belly, impossibly bright and charged with power. And now, no longer resisting the pull of the planet, hail began to fall in curtains and waves over the land.

Even over the crashes of thunder and the pounding of ice on river water and leaves, I could hear the panicked screams of the villagers as they ran for cover. The gardens were being torn apart.

I felt Laguna calling out to me and I called back. I tried to push off my branch, to take flight, to join her, but my talons wouldn't let go. I steadied myself with my wings and tried again. I was momentarily out of control of my own body, but—I realised in that instant—this *wasn't* my body. How *could* it be? I wasn't born with feathers and wings and hollow bones! These talons, holding on so tightly out of fear and panic didn't belong to me at all. This was all a lie. Only the water and electricity around me were real.

And Laguna, who I had somehow to reach if I was to survive.

I wanted to fly to her, but my senses were conflicted, and I was losing the moment. I could feel my mammal heat on ferns and the coolness of the cave all around me. I knew that I was trying to retreat from this world because I was scared and weak and wanted to be home—a single point of reference that I could clean and control and where nothing would change without my permission.

And in that final moment before I returned to my mammal body, I saw the lightning hitting the oily river with a crack and an explosion of fire.

I saw the chunk of white hail falling and smashing into Laguna's skull.

I felt my world ending once again.

epilogue

I've always struggled with the idea of feeling like part of something bigger than myself. There were a few times when I came close to understanding.

Moments during story time at the Sanctuary, when I'd looked around the dark office space at the humans gathered and felt some sense of belonging. And there had been a brief moment, during that demonstration on the day of the earthquake, where being in such a large crowd united by a purpose—no matter how vague—had made anything feel possible. But none of that compared to the intense sense of connection that came from the movement which culminated in the Bunker Blockades.

We felt infinite and stronger each day. Each one of us had heard a calling. We were a swarm, a herd. And that feeling of being caught up in the riptide of history left little room for ethical reflection.

Which was practical, it turns out, because what we decided was needed to save the world was much more than any of us could have prepared our souls for.

We were people who cuddled chickens while telling each other stories, people who spent two days relocating a mouse nest from a wall rather than putting down poison. Plotting murder was unthinkable to people like us. And yet that's precisely what we did as our love for life became stronger by the day. The Imperative coursed through us and whispered to our dreams.

Leaving Sam at home, I joined Heather on her crusade. We didn't create the timetable, another wave of disease—and protest—drove the billionaires underground and we were ready for them.

The blockades were simply the manifestation of a movement; bright and visible, but also ephemeral. They were the fleshy toadstool appearing overnight, while the network was always there, growing in the darkness, making connections, and digesting the waste of the past. Our shifted movement was a mycelial network which had already spread across the land.

Fruiting bodies never last long and, on some level, we knew the blockades wouldn't either. With enough resources and power, a person becomes almost immune to death. At some point, the billionaires would surely find a way out.

And, just as surely, there would be fewer of them. Their time locked underground in their hiding places gave us time to dissolve their power.

We took that space to start building in their absence.

For me, the blockades were a tiny death. There was an explosion of growth followed by the stench of trauma and decay as our networks fell apart and we turned the intensity of what we had done in on each other. The infighting was horrific.

Were the blockades strategy or revenge? The Shift had happened, and the effect was profound, but what we did with it was as messy and incomplete as we were. Each one of us defended our own interpretation. We were only just beginning to learn to listen again to the land—and each other—we still had so far to go.

Our political toadstool swelled, released its spores then collapsed in on itself, filling our forest with flies. Friendships had held our tissues together for an exquisite moment; then just as quickly they dissolved into cells and broken pieces of membrane.

But like all tiny deaths, I was changed by this one. There was cellular death, as there always is, but there was also rebirth. Our actions were an imperceptible part of ourselves out in the world, inspiring, creating and destroying.

In death we centred ourselves in the moment. In new life we breathed a sigh of relief.

I came back to my body. My mammalian self. Covered in sweat, my face wet with tears. My migraine had passed, and I sat up and looked at my home.

In Sasu, home is a verb. It is our deliberate actions that create safety and comfort but also the inherent protection of the place we love. It is the memories stored in each living object and the constantly changing community of organisms who create our habitat.

And this home had ended for me now. My cave had become past tense.

I dressed, picked up my bag, and left.

I knew that if I stayed inside, I would never move on. I knew that if I began to tap into the loss welling in my chest, I would collapse in on myself.

Instead, I turned away from my cave and faced the sea. My attention followed a single wave merging, disappearing, becoming ten other waves. Wave fronts, like lines on a page moved towards the shore, shrinking and reappearing, growing, and fading. Laguna's voice whispered to my memory: *never the same twice.*

I smiled at the recollection of that flight together and of my stubborn resistance to the changing wind. My heart dropped. As though only in recalling her, I felt her absence and I was filled with guilt for that split second of almost forgetting. The storm had moved on, but the air around me still felt charged. Then guilt too abandoned me, and I was left as just myself; my feet in the sand, a person who had been loved and changed forever.

Would I ever fly again? I promised myself that I wouldn't. The feeling of air through my feathers was something I only wanted to share with Laguna. Without her, it wouldn't make sense.

I whispered to the sea then, to the waves and the salt, the sand, and the crabs, to the gulls wheeling above and a cream butterfly caught in an invisible eddy of air. Be well, I wished them all. I will honour you. The words left my lips and I felt them received.

I turned towards the land and began my journey. One last time to the village, to say goodbye. One last look back so I could move forward.

* * *

Whatever I was expecting to find at the village, it was worse. My senses were slow to take in the charred houses and the tatters of bridges and ropes hanging between trees. Patches of black grass dotted the village circle where lightning had struck and the air smelled of jet fuel, of poison, of the leftovers of another age.

I walked across the village, automatically to where Laguna's house had once stood proud in the trees. In the shade of the wreckage, where the sun couldn't reach, hail lay as innocent as fresh snow among the vegetables, herbs and flowers torn from their vertical beds. There was no-one. I heard the gate to the chicken enclosure squeak open in the breeze but there was no contented murmuring of hens bathing in the sand. The village was abandoned and that made sense. *Who would stay here?*

But also, where would they go? My first thought was the airport— the only proper buildings within a day's walk. Then the memory of collapsing walls, dust and panicked pigeons returned. I looked around me. *Why does everything end like this?*

I walked through the broken pieces of wall and roof that were once Laguna's home. Jars spilled herbs out onto the grass and a soaked futon mattress, torn down the middle, released her secrets with its cotton fluff.

Now that I stood there among the devastation of the village, I began to realise how impossible the task of mourning all this was going to be. Part of me expected myself to simply curl up among Laguna's memories and magic and just die right there in the grass.

But I didn't, not yet. My body took over my decisions and led me to the storage tent, one of the only structures to have been left standing. Hail crunched underfoot as I stepped up to the door. It was open, I went inside. I had never seen it this empty. Even in the hard times, the villagers had always managed to keep something on the shelves, I had never once returned home from a raid empty-handed.

I took a moment to walk along the empty racks and suddenly the reality of needing to find my own food from that day on—to explore new places to raid, to collect, and hunt and go hungry more often than not, all felt insurmountable. Dying might be easier after all.

But then, at the back of the tent, my eyes fell upon a plastic box. I opened it and took in the sight of the food there, a thick chunk of bread and a whole nest of boiled eggs.

A shiver ran down my spine.

I ran out of the tent and looked up.

A clear sky. I was alone.

And yet.

Despite my own promises to myself, I changed form, I expressed. I left my human-self lying among the charred grass and piles of hail and I took flight.

Keeping my gaze fixed towards the horizon, I climbed higher than ever. I took in the distant line that marked the end of the forest and wetlands; the mountain range looking down over everything I had known for the last five years.

And then I saw them. The line of shadows moving towards the mountains and the future. A trail of people carrying backpacks. The silhouette of a human-person carried in a stretcher. Another shiver coursed through me, and this time I understood.

about the author

Kes Otter Lieffe is a writer, ecologist, and community organiser. She is the author of *Margins*, a trilogy of queer speculative fiction novels, several short stories, and a colouring book series on queer ecology. Kes writes from a working-class, chronically ill, transfeminine perspective.

www.otterlieffe.com